JUST JOKING!

Is this the right book for you?
Take the JOKING TEST and find out.

YES	NO	
❏	❏	Do you ever pretend that you are dead to get out of going to school?
❏	❏	Do you like to call up people you know and pretend to be someone else?
❏	❏	Do you leave banana skins in the middle of busy sidewalks?
❏	❏	Do you own any of the following items: fake dog poo, rubber vomit, gorilla suit?
❏	❏	Do you wish that every day could be April Fools' Day?

SCORE:	One point for each "yes" answer.
3–5	You are a practical-joking genius. You will love this book.
1–2	You are a good practical joker. You will love this book.
0	You are not a practical joker. You are what practical jokers call a "victim." You will love this book.

Also by Andy Griffiths

Just Annoying!
The Day My Butt Went Psycho!

ANDY GRIFFITHS

JUST Joking!

WITH ILLUSTRATIONS BY TERRY DENTON.

Scholastic Inc.

New York Toronto London Auckland Sydney
Mexico City New Delhi Hong Kong Buenos Aires

ISBN 0-439-42472-0

Text copyright © 1997 by Backyard Stories Pty. Ltd.
Illustrations copyright © 1997 by Terry Denton

All rights reserved. Published by Scholastic Inc.

SCHOLASTIC and associated logos are trademarks and/or registered trademarks of Scholastic Inc., 557 Broadway, New York, NY 10012.

12 11 10 9 8 7 6 5 4 3 2 1   3 4 5 6 7/08

Printed in the U.S.A.
First Scholastic paperback printing, December 2003

CONTeNTS

GREAT
FRESHWATER
FISH of the
WORLD #47

The
Thompson's
Gazelle.

...this page
is blank.

This should not be here.!!

PLAYING DEAD

It's 8:15 A.M. and I'm still in bed. I should have gotten up an hour ago.

But I didn't. You want to know why? Because I'm dead.

Well, not really dead. I'm just pretending I'm dead so I don't have to go to school.

If I can convince Mom and Dad that I'm dead, not only will I have pulled off one of the greatest practical jokes of the century, but I'll get off going to school for the rest of the year. Maybe even for the rest of my life.

I got the idea from my dog. I've been taking Sooty to obedience classes each

This is the start of the first story. We don't need any drawings here...

...or here.

...or here.

FRESHWATER
FISH of the
WORLD # 22:
The
doorhandle.
↓

Sunday morning. We've only been going for a few weeks, but already he's learned to sit, beg, *and* roll over. Yesterday he learned how to play dead. I thought, *If my dog is smart enough to do it, then why not me?*

All I've got to do is lie here without breathing or blinking. Well, when I say without blinking, I mean blinking when nobody is looking.

That's our son. When he died, we couldn't bear to part with him. So we had him stuffed & turned into a lamp.

And when I say without breathing, I don't mean not breathing at all — that would be stupid. I mean just taking a tiny little breath every so often — just enough to keep me alive.

The only thing that worries me is I'm such an excellent practical joker, I might kid myself into thinking I'm really dead. And if that happened, I'd be as good as dead — or as bad as dead — because as far as I can see, there's nothing really good about being dead, except that you don't have to go to school.

Suddenly Mom bustles into the room.

"What? Still in bed? Come on, you'll be late!"

Hello, I'm a pirahna

2

I hear the rattle of the curtains being opened.

The sudden light hurts my eyes, but I remember not to blink.

Any moment now, Mom is going to see me. And scream.

She's standing right next to me.

"Pooh, what a stink! When's the last time you cleaned this room? It's an absolute pig-sty! Dirty socks and undies everywhere. Why can't you put them in the laundry basket like your sister does? If you're not showered, dressed, and out of this house in ten minutes, you're going to miss your bus, and I'm not going to drive you."

She walks out of the room.

I stare at the ceiling. What else would a real corpse do? It's not as if it would make some brilliantly witty comeback, like "Lay off me, you old bag. I'm not going to school today because I'm dead. Just leave me alone so I can rot in peace." Yeah — that would be a good line, but I can't say it because I'm supposed to be dead. So, I just lie here and stare at the ceiling some more.

Next time your parents take you to a fancy expensive restaurant, have an eating race with your brothers/sisters. If the race is close, try stuffing food in your ears, up your nose, down your shirt, in the flower bowl or in your shoes.

JUST JOKING!

I'm sorry...the editor says that pirahna should be spelled PIRANHA. Excuse me!!

3

Next thing I know, Dad is standing next to the bed.

"Andy?" he says.

I don't answer.

"Are you all right?" says Dad in a slightly deeper voice.

I'm holding my breath. My body is tight.

He puts his hand on my shoulder and shakes me roughly.

"Andy!" he says. "Andy, I'm warning you . . . if this is another one of your practical jokes, it's not funny! You hear me? Not funny!"

I tense as hard as I can while Dad shakes me. Then he stops and puts his thumb and fore-fingers around my wrist. He's trying to find my pulse.

Darn! It's the one thing I can't fake. All the same, I try to concentrate on my heart and slow it down.

I read somewhere about these people who use the power of the mind to slow down their heartbeat, so I figure I might as well give it a try.

I imagine that my heart is as still as a rock. A red rock.

What is the next word in this series?

• FOOT
• LEG
• BACK
• NECK
• . . . .
Ans: Pg 24

APRIL 1ST should be WORLD PRACTICAL JOKING DAY

Try filling your parents' good work shoes/boots with warm custard. When they slip them on, say: "Happy World Practical etc Day" ! They'll love you

I guess that makes me a dumb piranha.

4

A paralyzed red rock.

A frozen paralyzed red rock.

A frozen paralyzed red rock in a deep, deep sleep.

It seems like forever, but eventually Dad puts my arm back down onto the bed. Gently.

And he says in a quiet voice: "Andy — now listen to me. You're cold and you're not breathing. You're staring at the ceiling and I can't find a pulse. You may be dead for all I know. But then your past record leaves me no choice but to wonder if this isn't just another one of your so-called 'jokes.' If you are just playing a trick, then I'll give you to the count of three to get out of bed and we'll say no more about it. But, if you don't get out of bed, and I find out later that you're not really dead . . . well, you'll wish that you had been. Is that clear?"

He's trying to trick me. He wants me to nod. But I'm not going to fall for it. There's only room for one practical joker around here — and it's not Dad. He starts counting.

DARE YOU TO STICK YOUR TONGUE IN THE END OF AN ESCALATOR.

"One . . ."

I'm not sure I believe that I won't get

so, why am I here?

5

into trouble if I confess. He sounds pretty serious. I'll probably end up being grounded for a week. And I'll *definitely* end up having to go to school.

"Two . . ."

What have I got to lose? And, anyway, I've come too far to chicken out now.

"Three!"

I don't move a single muscle.

Dad calls Mom into the room.

"Is everything all right?" she asks.

"I'm afraid I've got some bad news," says Dad. "I don't know how, or why, but it appears that Andy is no longer living . . . that is to say, he is . . . er . . . dead."

"Oh no," she says, and starts to cry. "Oh no!"

Out of the corner of my eye, I see Dad move to put his arms around her.

While they are distracted, I quickly take a couple of good deep breaths.

"But he was such a good boy!" Mom wails. "Such a *good* boy. He had his problems, but deep down he didn't mean any harm."

"No," says Dad, "I don't believe he did

Next time your friend is bragging, bet him he can't remove the cheese from a mousetrap with his nose. (Show him photos (fake) of you doing it)

Keep Hospital number close by.

I have to tell you the page number.

mean any harm — it's just, he never knew when to stop."

Dad's taking the whole thing better than I expected. I mean, he's usually pretty calm and all, but I would have thought, maybe, he might be a bit more upset. After all, I am his son.

"Oh well," he says. "No use standing around here all day. There's work to be done."

"But surely you're not going to work now!" says Mom.

"Well," says Dad, "somebody's got to dig the hole."

"What hole?"

"We can't just leave his body here."

"I suppose not," says Mom. "Where are you going to dig it?"

Dad hands her his handkerchief.

"I think underneath the lemon tree might be nice — and it'd be good for the lemons."

"Yes," says Mom, "it's been struggling a bit lately."

"I'll go get the shovel and start digging. I'd like to have him in the ground before lunchtime. Before he starts to smell."

"Okay," says Mom, wiping her eyes. "And

AMAZING
EYE
TRICK #1
↓
Stare at
this dot
●

■
and this
square
for 24 hrs,
with both
eyes closed
Which one
seems more
round?
Ans: pg 82

Dare you
to drop a
Red hot
Iron down
your pants.
IT WON'T
HURT.

7 Boredom
MAXIMOSO.

while you're doing that, I'll put the kettle on. I think we could both use a good strong cup of tea."

I can't believe what I'm hearing. Have my parents completely lost their senses? Are they seriously thinking of burying me in the back-yard? Aren't there laws against that sort of thing?

Dad leaves the room.

Mom kneels down beside the bed and kisses me on the cheek. She passes her hand over my eyelids, just like they do in the movies. I'm so touched, I almost forget to close them — but I remember just in time.

"I don't care what anyone says," she whis-pers. "You *were* a good boy."

Mom leaves the room.

I don't dare open my eyes again. I wouldn't want her to come back and catch me with them open. That would really freak her out. And I think she's been freaked out enough for one day.

Maybe I should confess.

But how do I confess without freaking her out even more? After all, if she thinks I'm dead and then I walk into the kitchen, what do I say?

THINGS
TO
DO:

Why not
try to
convince
your
brother
that
barbells
make
great
floaties.

FRESHWATER
FISH OF THE
WORLD #75:
Half of
something,
dunno
what!

8 This is page 8.
Get the idea?

Somehow, I don't think "Hi, Mom, I'm not really dead, I was just kidding!" would go down all that well.

FRESHWATER FISH of the WORLD #756:

The other half.

But if I don't confess, I'm going to be buried in a cold muddy hole in my own backyard.

I'll have worms gnawing at my eyeballs for the rest of eternity. That's a pretty high price to pay for a practical joke. Even one as brilliant as this.

The lemon tree is right outside my window. I can hear Dad digging. And whistling.

Whistling?

To discover the best practical joke ever, turn to Pg 130

I die and he whistles? What is he, some kind of psycho? Normal people don't whistle when their son dies. Then again, normal people don't bury bodies in the backyard.

But as I listen to Dad's whistle, I begin to notice something strange. It's different from his normal one.

It's too loud.

Too cheerful.

And now it becomes clear.

My parents don't think I'm dead — they just want me to think that they *think* I'm dead. All this stuff about being good for the

This is page 6 upside down.

9

lemons . . . that's not what it's about at all. They're just trying to teach me a lesson.

They want to scare me.

Well, I don't scare easily. And I'm not about to be beaten at my own game by a couple of amateurs.

Is your family COMPUTER KEYBOARD malfunctioning?

HOW TO FIX IT.

1. fill the bath with mud.

2. Screw off all bits that will screw off.

3. Carefully Chuck the keyboard and bits into the bath.

4. Stir with a tennis racket.

5. Glue all the bits together again with Craft Glue.

It should now work perfectly.

After a long morning of staring at the ceiling, I'm pretty bored.

At last I hear Dad stop digging.

Mom and Dad come into my room. I know what's coming next.

I suck my breath in and try to remain absolutely still. Dad grabs me underneath my arms. Mom lifts me up by the legs. I try to make my head flop around in a convincing corpse-like fashion. They carry me out to the backyard and lay me down underneath the lemon tree.

Dad gets down into the hole — which I can see through my slitted eyes is deeper than I expected — puts his hands back underneath my arms, and pulls me down toward him.

Hey, this is dinner.

10

My legs follow with a thud.

The mud at the bottom of the hole is cold and wet, and almost immediately my pajamas are soaked through. I'm sure Dad is just dying for me to crack and open my eyes so he can say, "Just kidding!"

A great thing to do on weekends (especially if you're bored) is to cram yourself in the bowl of your washing machine, preset the cold cycle, go to sleep!

But I'm not going to give him the pleasure. Not now . . . not ever.

Dad climbs out of the hole. Mom begins reading from a small blue book, her voice low and serious.

". . . Ashes to ashes . . . dust to dust . . ."

Dad is standing at attention, shovel by his side.

I'm starting to wonder if this is such a good idea after all. Dad starts filling in the hole. I don't have to wonder anymore — I know.

First I feel dirt hitting my toes. Then my legs, and then my stomach. A big clump lands on my chest and I feel dirt splatter onto my face and mouth.

Something's wrong. It's not possible that I'm such a brilliant actor that my parents really think I'm dead . . . is it?

Very tasty mosquito!!

No, that's stupid. . . . They'll crack . . . any minute now.

Another handful of dirt splashes across my face.

And another.

And now I don't know what to think because I'm almost completely buried and I'm having trouble breathing.

I open my mouth to shout, "Okay, you win! I was just kidding!"

But a big clump of dirt lands in my mouth and I can't get the words out.

Why the Long face?

It's dark.

It's quiet.

It's cold.

It's boring.

How long have I been here?

Am I dead?

If I am dead, then how come I'm still thinking?

I know one thing for sure. If I ever get out of this — and it's beginning to look like there's not

HEY YOU, MOUSE! Pull this handle.

I think the black thing just fell off the end of my nose.

much hope of that — I'm never going to play another practical joke for as long as I live.

Hang on, I can feel something on my stomach. Urgent jabbing and scratching. The weight of the dirt on my belly is lifting. When the scratching starts on my chest, I realize what it is.

Sooty has come to save me! He's the only one who realizes I'm not dead! He must be able to smell me, to sense my warmth.

And as the weight of the dirt lifts, I decide I don't care about playing dead anymore. Anything would be better than this. Even school.

I sit up and scream, "I confess! You win! I was just kidding!"

I wipe the mud out of my eyes and see my parents staring down at me.

They are shocked.

The sight of me rising from the dead has them goggling at me in horror, their mouths frozen open.

Mom starts screaming. Dad is trying to ward me off with his shovel, holding it in front of him, as if I'm some sort of zombie.

"Dad, it's okay!" I reassure him. "I was playing a dumb joke and I'm sorry!"

Before Breakfast Mechanical YOBA Exercise.

✩ Take your little brother's walkman or game boy.

✩ Poll it apart with screwdrivers hammers, & forklift truck

✩ Put all the bits in a crisp, new paper bag.

✩ Say: "Here, I fixed this for you!"

✩ RUN !!

But I might just as well be speaking another language.

My words don't seem to be having any impact on him whatsoever. He's still brandishing the shovel as he and Mom back slowly away from the hole.

This joke is completely out of control. The only one who's glad to see me is Sooty. He's standing at the top of the hole trying to lick my face. I push him away but he keeps coming back for more, like it's a game. At least somebody around here is acting normal.

Then, all of a sudden, Dad drops the shovel and clutches at his chest with his right hand. He drops to his knees, his mouth still wide open, then falls forward onto his face.

I leap out of the hole and rush to his side. I roll him over and check to see if he's breathing.

Nothing.

I place my hands on his chest and push with all my weight, just like they showed us in first aid. I push three more times. Then I pinch his nose and pull his head back.

NO MORE HEART ACHES!

NEW IMPROVED MECHO-HEART

SIMPLY SCREWS INTO CHEST & PLUG INTO LIVER. IT REALLY WORKS!

I'm about to start mouth-to-mouth resuscitation when Mom screams.

"Get away from him, you . . . you . . . *zombie!*"

"I'm not a zombie!" I tell her. "I'm not dead — I was just kidding!"

"Don't touch him, you bloodsucking freak!"

"Mom, I haven't got time to argue! I've got to do this. It's Dad's only hope."

I take a deep breath. Mom starts laughing. Poor Mom. The stress has affected her brain. And it's all my fault. But I can't help her until I've saved Dad. First things first.

I take another breath and am about to put my mouth over Dad's when he starts spluttering. First a sputter. Then a wheeze. And then a deep rocking laugh.

Dad opens his eyes. They are wet with tears.

"Would you mind sharing the joke with me?" I ask.

"Sure," says my father, pulling himself together with great effort. "We were *just kidding!*"

And then they really start to laugh. And laugh. And laugh.

BEAUTY TIP.

MIX IN SOME GLOW IN THE DARK PAINT WITH YOUR SISTER/BROTHER'S ACNE COVER-UP BEFORE THEIR BIG NIGHT OUT.

(In the disco their zits will glow like stars).

Page 3942.

15

HA

They're doubled over like a couple of maniacs. Even Sooty is rolling around on his back, wheezing and carrying on.

It takes a few moments for the shock to sink in, but then I realize that my parents have won.

I've been sucked in.

Sucked in, chewed up, and spat out.

But then, maybe things aren't as bad as they seem.

Never mind that I'm wet and cold.

Never mind that I'm covered in mud.

Never mind that I'm the victim of a heartless practical joke that had me thinking I had killed my father and driven my mother insane.

No, never mind all this.

At least I got the day off from school.

TRICK
YOUR DAD!
Tease his
nose hairs
& wax them
while he
is asleep.
He'll be so
grateful.

↓

Possible
shapes/
styles

Sorry, on that
last page N°
I made an error
of 3927.

16

GREAT
COCHROACH
HIDING PLACES
N° 7:
On a piece
of dental
floss.

Cockroach

You know, there's a world of opportunity out there," says Mr. Bainbridge. "A world full of opportunities just waiting for a young man like you. Yes, a world of opportunities!"

"Yes, sir."

I feel like taking the opportunity to tell him to shut up, but I'm much too polite for that. Besides, Mr. Bainbridge is Dad's boss.

I'm under strict instructions tonight to just sit quietly, behave myself, and not mess up in any way. The worst thing is, Dad has made me promise not to play any practical jokes.

No squirting flowers. No exploding cans of

peanuts. No rubber vomit.

Dad said that if I tried any funny stuff at the dinner table, my allowance would be stopped for a month.

I made the promise, but I don't think Dad realizes how hard it is for me. See, the thing is, I'm a practical-joke-a-holic. I need to play practical jokes like other people need to breathe air and drink water.

I don't really see what's wrong with a few harmless practical jokes, anyway. They help to break the ice. It's not like I've got a lot to say to Mr. and Mrs. Bainbridge.

I mean, how do you talk to people who think Ice-T is a drink? Or, that doing your homework is more important than figuring out how to defeat Sektor in Mortal Kombat 3?

And, as if that's not bad enough, what can you talk about with people whose eyes go all glassy when you try to explain these things to them?

What a snore-fest.

"Too many kids these days," says Mr. Bainbridge, "expect opportunity to come to them. But it doesn't work that way. Oh no.

...thank the sharks that last story finished...

You've got to go out and grab it by the neck. When I was a young man —"

"Dinner is served!" says Mrs. Bainbridge, coming into the room with an enormous bowl of salad.

"Thank God!" I blurt out, before I can stop myself.

"I beg your pardon?" says Mr. Bainbridge.

"Um, I just meant, um, let us be thankful to God for such a beautiful spread," I say quickly.

Mom and Dad are glaring at me.

"Oh," says Mr. Bainbridge, "that's all right then. For a moment there I thought you were taking the Lord's name in vain. That's the other trouble with young people today. They have no —"

"Perhaps you'd like to say grace, Andy?" says Mrs. Bainbridge. "The lasagna is getting cold."

"Oh, ah, yes," I say.

It's been so long since I said grace, I can barely remember the words.

Everybody closes their eyes.

For a moment I'm tempted to say, "Two, four, six, eight — dig in, don't wait!" but then I remember Dad's warning.

GREAT ROACH HIDING PLACES Nº42: on a tooth brush, between bristles and paste.

The fork!!

19

so far there have been 17 to's, two toos and one two in this story.

[count them!]

HA

"For what we are about to receive . . ."

I know I should have my eyes shut, too, but somebody's got to keep theirs open to make sure that everyone else's stay closed. And, as I'm the one saying grace, it might as well be me.

Did you say grace before you started spreading filth, Sidney?

But, as I'm trying to think of the next line, I see something in the salad bowl. Something oval. Something dark brown. Something that looks a lot like a dead cockroach.

At least, I think it's dead. It's sort of hard to tell. All I know is, there's a cockroach in the salad, and it probably wasn't put there on purpose. Unless Mr. and Mrs. Bainbridge eat cockroaches, which seems unlikely. I mean, Mr. Bainbridge must get paid more than Dad, and *we* don't have to eat cockroaches.

"May the Lord make us truly thankful. . . ."

Truly thankful for a cockroach?

This would be funny if it wasn't so serious.

I can't just put up my hand and say, "Excuse me, but there's a dead cockroach in the salad." It would make it look like the Bainbridges have a really dirty kitchen. They'd get really embarrassed because they'd

Pull!

I wonder what'll happen.

20

Now it's 22 to's, 3 too's and still only one two.

think that we think that cockroaches fall into their food all the time.

But even worse still, Dad might think that I put it there for a joke. And that would mean trouble.

GREAT COCKROACH HIDING PLACES Nº 12: Up someone's nose when they first wake up.

I have to get it out before anybody notices. For everybody's sake.

I grab my spoon to scoop the roach off the salad leaf. . . .

"Amen," says Mr. Bainbridge, finishing grace for me as he opens his eyes.

He picks up the salad bowl.

Q: Do you know the I.Q. of an average cockroach?
A: (a) 12 (see pg. 44)
(b) 120 (see pg. 98)
(c) 240 (see pg 122)

"Salad, Andy?"

"Yes, please," I say. Luck is running my way.

Mr. Bainbridge passes me the bowl. I scoop a large portion of salad onto my plate, including the top two pieces of lettuce with the dead roach in between.

So far so good.

Mrs. Bainbridge places a large slab of lasagna on the other side of my plate. Normally, my mouth would be watering, but the cockroach has kind of taken the edge off my appetite.

"Would you care for some potatoes, Andy?"

Mrs. Bainbridge passes me a bowl full of steaming spuds. I pick out one and pass the bowl to Mr. Bainbridge.

Now that the roach is on my plate, all I have to do is get it into my pocket before anybody notices.

But first I have to distract them.

"What a beautiful landscape!" I point to a painting on the wall above Mom's head.

Everybody turns to look.

I lift up the piece of lettuce. But the cockroach has other ideas.

It's not dead.

It jumps off the lettuce leaf onto the table and starts running.

Straight toward me.

The roach reaches the edge of the table and tumbles onto my lap. I try to brush it onto the floor, but it disappears underneath my napkin.

Luckily, the others are all still studying the painting. Nobody else has seen the roach's 12-inch sprint. I discreetly lift the corner of my napkin to see where the roach has gone, but it's not there. I feel a gentle

AMAZING EYE TRICK #2.

Stare at these 3 lines

| | |

through a magnifying glass.

Which one looks most like the emotion of envy?

Ans Pg 54.

22

prickling on my stomach. It's underneath my shirt!

I freeze. The roach crawls around my side and onto my back.

I guess I could crush it by throwing myself back hard against the chair. It would probably work, but it might take more than one try to actually kill it, and this could give Mr. and Mrs. Bainbridge the wrong impression. I don't want them thinking I've lost my mind.

"Are you interested in painting, Andy?" asks Mrs. Bainbridge.

what's worse than finding a cockroach in your salad?

"I like it," I say, "but I'm not very good at it." I'm trying hard not to panic.

"Ah!" says Mr. Bainbridge. "But practice makes perfect! If a fellow really wants to do something badly enough, and he's prepared to apply himself for long enough, then . . ."

"Yes dear," says Mrs. Bainbridge. "That's all very well, but perhaps Andy doesn't want to be a painter. What are your favorite subjects, Andy?"

I'm trying hard to concentrate on the conversation, but it's not easy. The roach has

SORRY,
the best
practical
joke ever
is really
on Pg 84

Answer
from Pg 4
• FOOT
• LEG
• BACK
• NECK
• DRAJB*

* Ancient
croat
word.
meaning
SMELLY
PIT DUG
IN THE
GROUND

relocated itself underneath my left arm. I can hardly breathe. It feels like it's burrowing into my armpit.

"I guess I like English the best. Not too crazy about math or science."

"No, no, no!" says Mr. Bainbridge. "You don't want to neglect your math and science. Keep your options open, that's what I say. Science and technology — that's where the opportunities are."

Mrs. Bainbridge rolls her eyes.

I'd feel sorry for her if I wasn't feeling so sorry for myself. I only have to put up with him for one night. She has to live with him.

The roach has finished playing in my armpit, and now I can feel it crawling down my chest. I can't stand it anymore.

That damn roach could be laying eggs in my belly button for all I know. They're probably incubating in my stomach right now. They'll hatch inside me and burst out of my chest, like the face-grabber in *Alien*.

I ask directions to the bathroom and excuse myself from the table.

It's roach-killing time.

flea
collar

Well, that was
educational.

24

42, 4, 2.
Count
them.

The bathroom is upstairs. I shut the door behind me and yank off my T-shirt. It flies across the room, skims the top of the toilet bowl, and lands in a heap beside it. But the roach is not on my chest.

GREAT
C/R
HIDEOUTS
Nº 81:
On the tip of a lipstick.

Or my back.

Uh-oh — not a moment to lose!

I kick my shoes off and peel off my pants and underwear in one swift movement.

I'm completely naked — except for my socks — but I still can't find the roach.

I bet there's a bucket waiting on the other side of this door.

There are only two places it can be, one of which is too horrible to even think about.

I study the pile of clothes carefully. The roach emerges from the bottom of my jeans. It's creeping up the left leg. I pick up one of my shoes. Very slowly, so that the roach doesn't notice, and raise it high above my head.

The roach reaches the bottom button of my fly.

I take a deep breath.

But something holds me back. If I smash it right there, I'm going to end up with its pasty white guts splattered all over

25

the front of my jeans.

Not cool.

Might look like I've had an embarrassing accident. I put my shoe down slowly. The roach crawls back inside my jeans.

There's got to be a better way than splattering.

I look around for inspiration.

There's a window above the toilet. It's high and very small, but it might do. I could climb up there, hold the jeans outside the window and shake the cockroach off.

No sweat. No splatter. No roach.

I pick up the jeans, taking care to hold the waist and the trouser legs closed so that the roach can't escape. I shut the lid of the toilet and use it to step up onto the toilet tank. The window is now level with my head.

I lean against the wall for balance and slide the window open as far as it will go. I push the jeans out of the window and shake them as hard as I can.

Suddenly, the roach is on my hand. I get such a fright, I drop the jeans, lose my footing, and crash down into the bathtub.

I feel like lying here, closing my eyes, and pretending it's all just a bad dream, but I have to find the roach before it disappears again. I get out of the bath and study myself in the mirror.

GREAT C/R HIDEOUTS Nº 37: Between the two tallest french fries.

The roach is sitting on top of my head.

This time I know exactly what to do. It's not going to be pleasant, but it's the only way. This is one tricky cockroach and I can't afford to take any chances.

No way am I going to fall for that one.

I go back to the toilet and get down onto my knees. I lift the lid and bend lower and lower until my head is right inside the bowl. Then I take a deep breath, reach up, and flush the toilet.

It's horrible.

Toilet water up my nose.

Toilet water in my ears.

Toilet water in my mouth.

Finally, the flushing stops. I sit back up.

It's gone.

But so are my jeans.

I can't go back to the table without them. What would I say? I can just imagine the conversation:

Blank.

MRS. BAINBRIDGE: Where are your pants, Andy?

ME: Oh, I accidentally dropped them out of the bathroom window, Mrs. Bainbridge.

MR. BAINBRIDGE: Isn't that annoying! It happens to me all the time. Why don't you have a look in my wardrobe and see if there's anything there that fits you?

Yeah, right. Dream on. Meanwhile, back in the real world, I'm naked from the waist down.

There's no choice, really, but to climb out the window and get my jeans. I'd rather not go a month without my allowance.

I climb back on top of the toilet tank and lean across to the tiny window. It's going to be a tight squeeze, but since I haven't eaten any dinner yet, I reckon I'll make it.

I grip the narrow ledge and pull myself up and halfway out.

It's a long way to the ground. I didn't realize I was so high up.

But I'm in no danger of falling.

I'm stuck.

I can't go forward and I can't go back.

And to make matters worse, there's

60, can you believe that? 5, 3. Wow!

someone banging on the door.

"Someone's in here!" I yell.

"Is everything all right?" calls Mom. "You've been in there an awfully long time!"

"Yes," I call. "I'll be out in a second."

"He's not answering!" says Mom. "I think there's something wrong!"

She can't hear me because my head is outside the house.

Then I hear Mr. Bainbridge's voice.

"Stand back, everyone. I'm going to break the door down."

Oh great. My hero.

I hear a huge crash.

Mr. Bainbridge is no muscle man, but the flimsy lock snaps like Arnie Schwarzenegger himself is out there.

"Oh my God!" says Mr. Bainbridge.

For probably the first time in his life, Mr. Bainbridge has taken the Lord's name in vain, but I guess the last thing he expected to see was my bare butt staring at him from his bathroom window.

"Oh my God!" says Mrs. Bainbridge.

"Oh my God!" says Mom.

"Oh my God!" says Dad.

"I know this seems a little unusual," I yell, "but there's a perfectly reasonable and logical explanation! See, while I was saying grace, I saw this cockroach in the salad bowl, only I didn't want to say anything because . . ."

But I might as well be telling it to the man in the moon.

Mom and Dad and the Bainbridges are too busy babbling on about ladders and firefighters and irresponsible young idiots who can't even be trusted to sit the right way on a toilet seat.

I close my eyes and wonder if I'll be able to interest anybody in bidding for the TV, newspaper, magazine, film, and book rights to my story, and whether the proceeds will make up for the allowance I'm about to lose.

One door closes, another opens.

Like Mr. Bainbridge says, there's a world of opportunities out there.

DANGEROUS COCKROACH HIDING PLACES.

1. Between cracker + cheese.

2. Between eyelid & eye.

3. On the blades of a food processor.

...this story ends here

...go on to next story

68 to's, 6 too's and only a miserly 3 two's. Wow, statistics can be so interesting.

Gorillagram

I have long, shiny black hair and big gray feet with black toenails. I have enormous hands with big stubby fingers. I have a spiky black mohawk, a big flat nose, and a mouth that moves.

Normally, you would find a creature like me in the jungle or in a zoo, but tonight I am loose on Lygon Street.

I am headed for a restaurant called La Trattoria, where Jen, my sister, is having her sixteenth birthday party.

If you didn't know I was wearing a gorilla suit you would swear that I was a real gorilla. That is, until I start dancing and singing "Happy Birthday."

Real gorillas don't sing "Happy Birthday."

Real gorillas don't sing much at all.

Not the ones I've seen in the zoo, anyway. I guess there's not much to sing about when you're stuck in the same cage day after day with all these human beings sticking their noses into your business.

A GORILLA?
↓

No...
Pete
Bronson
who lives
3 doors down
from me.

There's not that much to sing about when you're stuck in a gorilla suit, either.

It's a pretty weird experience. You feel sort of cut off from the world. It's like you're there but not there at the same time.

And to make things worse, the suit is about ten sizes too big.

I've only had it on for ten minutes and already I'm boiling hot. I can't see properly because the mask keeps falling forward over my eyes. I have to keep pulling it back against my face, which is a pain because the inside is already slimy with sweat and stinks of rubber.

Gorilla
pretending
to
be an
incinerator.
(Tricked me)

Everybody I pass either stares or waves at me. They're all trying to figure out what a gorilla is doing on Lygon Street. To tell you

I'm a new fish.

the truth, I'm starting to wonder myself.

At last I come to the restaurant, but I can't open the door. My hands are swimming in these big rubber gorilla gloves.

AMAZING EYE TRICK#1: Stare at this spot

●

for twenty minutes with your left thumb in your right nostril. Now, does this page appear to be 3D. No? It didn't for us, either.!!

Luckily, one of the waitresses opens it for me. I feel like I should say thank you, but I can't because real gorillas don't speak English.

The restaurant is full of people. They all turn to look at me.

Jen's party is on the second floor. I pull my mask back tight across my face for the five thousandth time and hunch over to the spiral staircase in the middle of the room. I pass a woman in a purple dress who says to her friends in a know-it-all voice, "It's just a gorillagram."

Talk about a party pooper.

The staircase is difficult to climb because my feet are so large and the steps are so small. When I get to the top, I look across the restaurant at Jen's table. She's sitting with her back to me.

A very rare steak, indeed.

I creep up behind her and put my paws over her eyes.

The other one was so boring. We had him replaced.

33

"Who is it?" she asks.

I don't say anything.

"Come on," she says, trying to pull my hands away. "I give up."

I crouch down, put my head close to hers, and take my hands away.

She screams.

A GORILLA? ↓

No, my third grade teacher

I jump up and start dancing around the table. I can't see properly. The inside of the mask is dripping with perspiration.

All I can taste is rubber.

I bump my knee on the corner of the table. It hurts bad but I don't stop dancing.

I start singing a version of "Happy Birthday" without words — just grunts.

Everybody is laughing. Jen's friends, Mom and Dad, the people at the surrounding tables — everybody, that is, except Jen.

Mechanical Martini

"I know it's you, Andy," she says. "You're an idiot! Go away!"

When I finish singing, I go up and put my arm around her. I growl really loudly and give her a big sloppy kiss on the cheek.

"Get lost!" she says. "I mean it!"

But I'm just starting to enjoy myself. I put

Do you like my hat?

my hand into her plate of spaghetti and pretend to scoop it into my mouth, but I deliberately miss and smear it all over my face. Jen is not impressed.

"Get out of my dinner!" she says. "I can't eat that now. Why do you have to wreck everything?"

AUSTRALIA should become a BANANA Republic...

GORILLA trying to impersonate Politician.

She picks up the whole bowl and tips it over my head. Strands of spaghetti and tomato sauce slide down in front of my eyeholes.

But I don't get mad.

I grab a glass of water, drink a big mouthful, and, standing on one leg with my arms out to the side — like a fountain — I begin to squirt the water through my teeth. All over Jen. She starts screaming at me.

"Andy — that's enough!"

That's Mom. And she means it.

Time to split.

I put my arms over my head, like I know I've been a very naughty gorilla, and skulk toward the stairs.

I forget that my feet are too big for the steps and end up in a heap at the bottom.

Not a very dignified exit, but a gorillagram

Oi! Who took my hat?

they'll never forget.

I pick myself up off the restaurant floor as if nothing out of the ordinary has happened — as if this is the way gorillas always come downstairs.

Some women are watching me and smiling. One of them is the woman in the purple dress.

A GORILLA? ↓

No, it's the local TRAFFIC OFFICER (Hates skateboards)

Just a gorillagram, eh?

I lope up to their table like I'm the sweetest, meekest gorilla on Earth, just coming up to have my head scratched. Then, without warning, I raise my arms and roar as loudly as I can. They all jump back in fright.

It works better than I'd expected.

In fact, they get such a fright that I get a fright myself. With my heart racing, I make it back out onto the street.

You don't want CRAYFISH. No.No. It's not nice this time of year

I was going to go back to the car and change, but I'm too pumped up. This suit has powers I never even dreamed of.

There is a seafood restaurant next door to La Trattoria. Everybody is staring at me through the glass. It's weird. I'm feeling less and less like a human being.

KNOCK KNOCK

That's better.

This must be what it feels like to be one of the gorillas at the zoo — being stared at all day long. People watching you eat. People watching you go to the bathroom. People watching you while you're trying to watch TV.

Except for one important difference: I'm outside on the street, free. The human beings are the ones who are trapped.

I start to imagine that I have just escaped from the zoo and that I am seeing the street and its inhabitants for the first time, as if the human world is the zoo and I am the visitor.

New Gorilla head bowling balls.

I move up to the window and press my face against it.

I start staring back at the humans — pointing and poking my finger against the glass.

The humans are not quite sure how to take this. Some smile. Others just stare back blankly. They're not used to being watched.

An old man and lady are sitting at the table nearest the window. They are not taking any notice of me. I ignore the other patrons and study the old couple intently.

They just keep eating and talking, as if I'm not there.

I break off a couple of twigs from a tree on the edge of the sidewalk and hold one in each hand.

As the old man cuts his food with his knife, I cut an imaginary plate of food with my twig. As he puts the food into his mouth with his fork, I put the imaginary food into my mouth with my other twig.

A GORILLA?
↓

No.. close though. It's our school principal.

The man looks at me. He says something to the old lady. She looks at me and waves her hand dismissively.

I ask myself what a real gorilla would do in this situation and the answer comes to me.

I turn around, bend over, and moon them. I hoot loudly and run down the street to the next restaurant.

I can't stop laughing.

That old couple will probably spend the rest of their lives wondering why on earth they were mooned by a gorilla.

This is more fun than gorillagrams. I am a gorilla with a get-out-of-zoo-free card, and I'm not going to waste a second.

KNOCK KNOCK

It's like dog poo.

At the next restaurant, I don't press my face against the glass. I don't imitate anybody. I just stand gawking.

After a few minutes, one of the waiters comes out. He seems a little nervous.

"Um, er, ah . . ." he says in a shaky voice. "Can I help you?"

I cock my head to the side, as if I don't understand.

"Can I help you?" he asks again after a long pause.

I step toward him.

He steps back.

I grunt.

"I'm sorry, sir, but I really must ask you to move away from the window or I will have to call the police."

I grunt again and step closer to the little man. He stands his ground.

I reach out and give him a big hug.

But he doesn't freak out. He hugs me back. The people inside the restaurant applaud.

I grunt, release the waiter, and pat him on the head. Then I give a low bow, turn around, and walk down the street.

I'm having such fun visiting all the restaurants along Lygon Street, I lose track of the time.

I'm not sure how much later it is when I return to the seafood restaurant. The old man and lady are gone, but a couple of girls are sitting at their table.

A GORILLA?
↓

I put my hands up behind my head, start swiveling my hips and singing, "I'm too sexy for my gorilla suit."

I'm dancing pretty well I think — for a gorilla — but the girls are not interested. They are looking at something behind me.

That's when I notice the flashing blue light reflecting off the restaurant window.

No, wrong again!!
It's a gorilla's reflection

I turn around. There are two police officers, a man and a woman, crouched beside a police car.

Uh-oh.

The man is talking into the handpiece of his radio. The woman is holding a tranquilizer gun. The dart is pointed at me.

Time to become human again.

"Don't shoot!" I yell. "I'm not a real gorilla! It's just a suit!"

KNOCK! KNOCK!

That's better.

The policewoman brings her left hand up to her tranquilizer gun so that now she is holding it with both hands.

"Stay there, big fella!" she says. "Don't move. Everything will be all right."

"No, you don't understand," I say. "You're making a terrible mistake!"

~POP~

New all electric Gorilla. (very handy)

But either she's not listening or my voice is muffled by the mask, because she keeps that thing pointed right at my chest.

I realize that the quickest way to convince her that I'm not a gorilla would be to take my mask off.

I grab the hair on top of my mask and pull. But it won't come off.

I can't undo the ties that attach the back of the head to the suit because my hands are inside the big rubber gloves. And I can't get the gloves off because I need the use of my fingers to undo the press-studs on the cuff.

Typical Gorilla paw prints. (This one's wearing high heels)

"Come on," I say. "I know it looks real, but it's just a suit, okay? Just a dumb gorilla suit."

"Okay, boy," says the policeman. "It's okay. We don't want to hurt you. Just want to

41

Page 41, by the way. And where's my hat?

get you back to the zoo where you belong."

"I don't belong in the zoo!" I yell. "I'm a human being! I'm wearing a suit, but I can't get it off!"

The police look at each other. They frown.

"What do you think he's trying to say?" says the policewoman.

A GORILLA?

No, it's a dog, idiot!!

"I don't know, but he sure seems to be trying to tell us something."

"Almost human, aren't they?"

"Yeah, it's scary."

"I am human, you idiots!" I bellow.

Then I have a brainstorm. I'll sing "Happy Birthday." That will prove beyond a doubt that I'm not a gorilla.

I start singing at the top of my voice.

"Why is it making that horrible noise?" says the policewoman.

"I'm not sure," says the policeman. "Sounds like it's in pain."

I hear applause and laughter coming from the other side of the street. A large crowd has formed. And Jen is among them! Thank goodness!

"Jen!" I call. "Jen! Help me!"

Charles DARWIN and his MOM.

42

Thank you, dog breath!

She doesn't move.

"Jen!"

I jump up and down and point to her.

"That's my sister!" I say to the officers. "Ask her! She'll tell you I'm not a gorilla!"

But Jen makes no attempt to come across to me. She just stands there scowling, her arms folded.

"Excuse me, are there any stories about Mechanic birds in this book?

"Excuse me, miss," calls the policewoman. "This might be a silly question, but do you know this gorilla? He seems to know you."

Jen looks me up and down.

She hasn't forgiven me for the gorillagram, or for what I did to her spaghetti.

In fact, it was probably Jen who called the police.

No, BACK OFF.

I know she'll help me, but it will take some serious sucking-up.

"I'm sorry for the gorillagram, Jen," I call. "I didn't mean to mess up your party. I'll make it up to you, I promise. Anything you want. I'll give you money. I'll be your slave for a week. I'll give you all my Easter eggs next Easter. You name it, it's yours. Can you just tell these police that it's me? Come on,

BAD Mr Cockroach

SPLAT!!

diaper

Now I can smell baby poo.

43

Jen, please . . . this is serious!"

But my words are drowned out by the roar of a large green truck with ZOO painted on its side. The truck screeches to a stop behind the police car.

A group of zookeepers armed with nets and tranquillizer guns pile out of the back.

"Well?" says the policewoman to Jen.

"Now, Jen, now! Tell her!" I call.

Jen shakes her head.

"Are you kidding?" she says. "I've never seen it before in my life."

A dog?

↓

WOOF WOOF

o, it's a gorilla pretending to be a dog.

If you think the IQ of a cockroach is so low, how come I've got you running around this book trying to find the answers to meaningless questions?

oh very funny. How humiliating. A baby's diaper on my head. Well, I am a bit hungry. Yum Yum!!

Nick-knockers
Anonymous

Thursday night.

Mom and Dad have gone out and left me at home all by myself.

Normally, I would be making prank phone calls, setting up buckets of water over half-opened doors, and putting rubber snakes underneath pillows — but not tonight.

Tonight I'm standing on a ladder polishing the lightbulbs in the living room with Dad's CD cleaning cloth.

Don't tell me. I know what you're thinking. You're thinking, *Andy, if your parents really have gone out and left you all alone, why are you wasting precious practical joke preparation time polishing lightbulbs? Why aren't you making prank phone calls, setting up buckets of water over half-opened doors, and putting rubber snakes underneath pillows?*

Well, the reason is that tonight I've decided to clean up the house as a surprise for Mom and Dad. I'll admit, it might seem a bit unusual to polish lightbulbs, but the trick to making a place look really clean is in the details. And believe me, I have to make this place look *really* clean.

See, Mom and Dad have gone to my school for parent–teacher conferences, and I already know that my reports are not going to be that great. Lousy, in fact.

A bucket of 3 week old whale vomit, He He

It's not my fault, though. I've worked really hard this year, but my teachers are all against me. They think that just because I spend a lot of time talking and laughing in class, I'm not concentrating. But what they don't realize is, I can't help talking and laughing in class because I get so excited about schoolwork. I've tried to explain this to them, but they won't listen. It's like I said,

New fish. The other one's sick. Must've been something he ate.

they're all against me.

So what I've decided to do is clean up the house and make it absolutely soil-free and spotless, right down to the very last lightbulb. That way, when Mom and Dad come home fuming about my lousy reports and launch into their "it's time we had a little talk" routine, they're suddenly going to be struck by how beautiful the house is looking, and they'll forget all about lecturing me.

They'll be so impressed that I cleaned up the house without being asked, that, as a reward, they'll let me eat a whole bucket of chocolate ice cream and stay up till midnight watching TV. It's a lucky thing for me that my parents are so gullible; otherwise I might have been in a lot of trouble.

I'm halfway through polishing the second lightbulb on the chandelier. There's a knock on the door. It can't be Mom and Dad because they're not due back for at least half an hour.

I climb down the ladder and open the front door. But there's nobody there.

"Hello!" I call. "Hello?"

Page 47

No answer.

That's strange. Whoever it was must be really impatient. I hate that.

I close the door, climb back up the ladder and continue polishing the lightbulb.

There's another knock at the door.

"Hang on," I yell, "I'll be right there."

I practically jump off the ladder and rush to the door.

I open it.

Nobody there.

This is obviously somebody's idea of a joke. And I can guess exactly who that somebody is — Danny Pickett.

Poor Danny. That guy is a compulsive nick-knocker. He can't bear to walk past a house without knocking on the front door and running away. I reckon he should join Nick-knockers Anonymous.

He's probably out in the yard somewhere right now, laughing at me.

"Danny!" I call. "You might as well come out. I know it's you."

I peer into the darkness but I can't see him anywhere.

Page 49.

"Okay," I say, "have it your way."

One last scan of the yard and I close the door. Let him freeze if he wants.

I've hardly put my foot on the first rung of the ladder when he knocks again. But this time, I don't answer it.

He knocks again. And again.

I climb to the top of the ladder and start polishing the third lightbulb. I concentrate on it to help block out the sound of the knocking.

LADIES who desire access to the best practical joke ever!! Be QUICK! Do not delay. TURN TO Pg 9.

It's actually a very interesting lightbulb. An Osram. Sixty watts. Clear. A little squiggly thing in the middle. Ouch. It hurts to look at the little squiggly thing for too long.

Danny's still knocking, but I'm not going to open the door. It will only encourage him and make me look like an idiot. He can knock until his knuckles are red-raw and he's bleeding to death right on our front doorstep. See if I care.

C'mon puss Hungry puss Eat the nice food

Yeah, see if I care.

I don't care. . . .

Yes I do! I do care!

It's driving me crazy!

Page 52.

He knocks on and on and on. He's not going to stop until I open the door.

I jump off the ladder, sprint to the door, and open it — all in one fluid movement. I'm going to catch him and kill him. But even before I open the door, I know I'm too late.

He's gone. Nobody but the wind. A flurry of brown autumn leaves blows through the door and onto the carpet — the carpet that I vacuumed only fifteen minutes ago. I slam the door.

This means war. I'll be ready for him next time. Danny's fast on his feet, I'll give him that. But when it comes to brainpower, he's no match for me.

I go to the laundry room and grab the yellow plastic bucket. I take it back to the kitchen and fill it about halfway with white flour. I put the bucket on the table and go into the pantry. I take out a bottle of tomato sauce, a bottle of soy sauce, a jar of blackberry jam, a can of tomato paste, a jar of corn relish, a bottle of vinegar, a can of spaghetti, a jar of peanut butter, a dozen eggs, a jar of honey, a box of cornflakes, and a small jar of crushed chili peppers.

I put all the ingredients into the bucket and start mixing them up with a wooden spoon. It's hard work because the mixture is so heavy and gloppy.

I add heaps of water and mix the sludge around and around. That's better. And now I have a whole bucketful of the stuff.

-Mouth
Open...

C'mon
Snore!
SNORE!!

I can't wait to see Danny's face when, just as he's about to knock, I whip open the door and throw all this in his face. That should cure him of nick-knocking, once and for all.

After about ten minutes of mixing, there's still a lot of lumps, so I get out the electric blender and pour some into the jug. I turn it on high.

Suddenly, there's reddish-black stink-sauce everywhere. All over me, and all over the kitchen.

I forgot to put the lid on the blender. I hate that.

Once it's all pretty-well mixed, I carry the bucket up the hall to the front door. The bucket's so full and the mixture's so runny that

OK.. OK..
Pg 51.

51

no matter how slowly I walk, it spills over the sides, all the way up the hall. Never mind — plenty of time to clean that up after I've dealt with Danny.

I set the bucket down on the carpet and crouch down to wait.

Danny will be back any minute now. I know Danny. He thinks that if something is funny once, then it will be a thousand times funnier if you do it a thousand more times.

I know how he thinks. He'll figure I've left the door by now. But he's wrong — I'm here, waiting.

I'll hear him step onto the porch. I'll hear him open the screen door. And just before he knocks, I'll open the door and give him a bath.

The house is very quiet, except for the sound of the trees brushing against the roof.

I've got my ear pressed up against the crack of the front door so I can hear even the tiniest movement on the veranda.

I hope he comes soon. The sludge is making my eyes water. I need to get a clothespin to put over my nose, but I don't dare leave the front door. Timing is crucial.

52

A mosquito buzzes around my head. I grab at it, but I miss and it flies up toward the hall light. I start to get up to have another try at it when I hear a footstep on the veranda. I crouch back down.

More footsteps. He's coming all right.

I move my hand up to the doorknob. I'm so wound up, I'm shaking. I've got to get this exactly right.

I strain to hear him. Another footstep. He must be at the screen door now. It creaks as he opens it.

I can see him in my mind's eye — in slow motion — pulling the door open. Curling the fingers on his left hand into the knocking position. Drawing his hand back. Stifling a giggle with his other hand as he raises his arm, ready to strike.

That's it. Now!

I open the front door and heave the contents of the bucket onto Danny. It's a perfect throw. I've caught him red-handed. He's covered in the stinking gooey brew. I can't even see his face. Revenge!

He gasps and wipes some of the chunky

I'm really a Mexican walking fish...

stew out of his eyes.

I realize I've made a terrible mistake.

It's not Danny.

"Mom?" I say.

She gasps again.

AMAZING EYE TRICK #2 ANSWER:

None look like envy. They're just ink lines, OK!! DUMMY.

This is not good. And to make things worse, Dad appears behind her.

"What's going on?" he says, looking at Mom and then at me.

"Um, er . . ." I say. That's all I can think of. Pretty pathetic really.

The mixture is everywhere. All over the entrance hall, all over the screen door, and all over Mom. She's standing there looking like the creature from the black lagoon. The goo slides off her clothes and collects in a puddle at her feet.

She is just gasping and shaking her head. Nothing in all her years of putting up with my jokes has prepared her for this.

"I think we need to have a little talk," says Dad softly. He appears calm, but his ears are very red, and they're trembling — that's not a good sign.

Not that I'm worried.

...but I'm trapped inside this ugly piranha's body.

Any minute now they're going to notice the inside of the house and see how clean it is. Except for the kitchen, of course. And the sludge on the hall carpet and around the entrance. But that's easily fixed. Once they notice the lightbulbs they'll calm down.

Any minute now I'll have them eating out of the palm of my hand. Any minute now. It's just a matter of time.

TELL YER MOM i SAVED YA!

i'm standing right on the edge of this huge boulder, looking over Sealers Cove on one side – where we camped last night – and Refuge Cove on the other. There's a cool breeze. I close my eyes and imagine I'm the last person on Earth. It's so peaceful. A three-night hike in Wilson's Promontory can be hard work, but it beats school any day.

Suddenly, I feel a large hand clamp down on each of my shoulders. I'm shoved forward. My stomach drops. My life starts to flash before my eyes. Then, just as suddenly, the hands pull me back.

"Tell yer mom I saved ya!"

I turn around. Roseanne O'Reilly is grinning widely.

"You idiot!" I shout. "What a dumb trick! I could have been killed!"

OH— MY favorite blood group.

"It's lucky I was here to save you then," she says. "You should be thanking me."

"Thanks for nothing," I say.

It's a typical Roseanne joke. Dumb and dangerous. She's been pulling this trick on everybody since we left Tidal River yesterday morning. It's her first time hiking. I think she's a bit overexcited. She's new to the school. I don't know why she decided to join the hiking club. Probably because no other club would have her.

For advice on how to fix a blister on the toe, turn to pg 65

O'Reilly swaggers back to the trail where the rest of the group are resting against their backpacks.

"You should have seen Andy's face," she announces to the party. "I really had him scared!" Not that anybody cares. They're as sick of Roseanne as I am.

Danny comes over.

"Trail mix?" he says.

whew... back again... thought I'd got lost.

He hands me a plastic bag full of chocolate chips, oats, peanuts, and sunflower seeds. I take a big handful and pass the bag back. My hands are still shaking from the fright.

"Don't feel bad," he says. "Roseanne punched me in the nose this morning."

"Really?" I say. "Why?"

The author recommends to anyone wishing to get more out of this story, the placing of a plastic bucket over your head, while reading!

WOW!!

"She asked me if I wanted to smell some cheese. Before I could answer, her fist was right in front of my face, and then **POW!**"

"She didn't wait for your answer? That's not a practical joke – it's just a punch in the face!"

"Tell me about it," says Danny. "She made my nose bleed, too."

"What did you do?"

"Nothing. She's bigger than me."

"Good point. But we can't let her walk all over us like this. We've got to get her back. Got to teach her a lesson."

"Sure," says Danny through a mouthful of trail mix. "But how?"

I sit on the boulder and use a twig to pry a pebble out of the tread on my boots. Suddenly, the answer is clear.

TRAIL
MIX

↓

one of my legs has been bitten off!!

"I know," I say. "Rocks!"

"Rocks?" says Danny.

"We'll put rocks in her backpack! That'll give her something to laugh about."

"Great idea," says Danny, "but how are you going to get the rocks into her backpack without her seeing?"

"I'm not going to put the rocks in her pack," I say. "You are."

"Me?" says Danny. "What if she catches me?"

"She won't," I say, "because I'll divert her."

There are three rocks — each roughly the size of a small coconut — a few yards down the trail. I point them out to Danny.

"Those will do."

"All of them?" says Danny.

"All of them. And hide them down in the bottom of her pack so she doesn't find them until tonight."

"Hang on," says Danny. "Which one is Roseanne's pack?"

"It's a blue MacPac," I say.

I look around for Roseanne. She's over ear-bashing Derek Watson, the leader of the trip. She has her compass out and is

Urban
Trail
Mix

Fresh
butts
with
french
flies.

59

It was my favorite one, too... my right leg.

pointing it toward the ocean. Derek is shaking his head. Her first hike and already she thinks she knows better than the leader! She is really something else.

Roseanne has this brand-new compass, which she hasn't stopped showing everybody for the whole trip. She's got no idea how to use it, but that doesn't stop her from telling everybody else how to use theirs. It gives me an idea.

Wow. a sandwich

"Hey, Roseanne," I say. "Can you give me some help checking my compass? I'm not sure if it's pointing true north or not."

She's already on her way over. We go back to the boulder and start comparing compasses, taking sightings on one of the small, rocky islands out from the coast.

BURP!

I stall her for about ten minutes and then return to the group. Danny nods and winks.

People are getting ready to move. I sit down and slip my arms through the straps of my backpack. It weighs a million tons. I packed food for four days, but it feels like I've got enough to last for the next four months. Maybe I shouldn't have brought so

This mosquito won't eat for months now.

Although, for you, it's on the left-hand side.

much canned food.

But I don't mind. No matter how heavy my pack is, Roseanne's must be even heavier.

Not that it seems to be giving her much trouble. She picks it up with one hand, slips her arms through the shoulder straps and strides to the front of the group. She's off down the trail and around the bend before anybody else has even started walking. You'd think Danny had filled her pack with helium balloons.

Even though my legs are feeling like jelly after the morning's climb, I walk quickly to catch up with Roseanne. I want to enjoy the sight of her carrying our rocks. If nothing else, it'll help take my mind off the weight of my own load. No matter how much pain I'm in, she'll be feeling worse.

She's walking so fast that after about fifteen minutes, we've left the rest of the group way behind. The trail becomes steeper and slightly overgrown. Roseanne pushes her way past a small tree branch that's hanging across the track and holds it back for me.

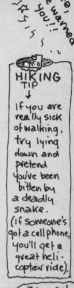

See! We warned you!!

HIKING TIP
↓
If you are really sick of walking, try lying down and pretend you've been bitten by a deadly snake. (If someone's got a cellphone, you'll get a great helicopter ride).

They want to know what kind of chopper you want.

Left-FOOT side, I meant to say

A GUIDE TO COMMON ROCKS FOUND ON HIKING TRAILS

1. A Rock

2. Square Rock

3. Pointy Rock

4. Spotty Rock

5. Small Rock

6. BIG ROCK

7. Flat Rock

8. WOMBAT ROCKS (Edible).

Just as I'm about to grab it, she lets go and the branch flicks back hard against my face. The pain makes my eyes water.

"Watch it," I say. "Are you trying to blind me?"

"Sorry about that," says Roseanne. "But you should always try to keep at least two yards behind the person in front so that they can't flick branches in your face."

"I *was* staying behind, but you deliberately held it back for me."

"That's 'cause I'm such a nice person," she says. "I thought you'd grab it. Honest!"

"Yeah, right, Roseanne."

She must think I was born yesterday. She's staring at me with that stupid grin on her face. And, what's worse, she doesn't look the slightest bit tired. There's not a single drop of sweat on her.

"How are you feeling?" I ask.

"Great!" she says. "How about you?"

"Fine!" I say. "Never felt better. You've got such a big backpack, though. It looks like it must be heavy."

"Yeah, it's heavy," she says. "But I can handle it. Hey, what's that on your sweater?"

62

Now, they've both gone !! ARGHHH!!

She points to my chest.

I freeze. Please, oh please, don't let it be a spider. Anything but a spider. I look down and Roseanne flicks her finger up my chin, my nose, and off the top of my head.

"Gotcha!" she cackles, as I jerk backward, which is not a good move, considering how heavy my pack is. The next thing I know, I'm falling off the trail and crashing through the brush.

I'm in a thornbush. I can't get up. I'm on my back, just like an upside-down tortoise.

"Enjoy your trip?" calls Roseanne.

"Shut ya face," I say.

"Are you all right?"

"I don't know," I say. "I can't get up."

"Hang on," she says. She shrugs off her pack and slides down the bank commando-style. "Give me your hand."

The thought of having to hold Roseanne's hand is only marginally more appealing than having to hold a live spider, but I'm not exactly in a position to refuse.

Her grip is strong and she pulls me up easily. But I can't put any weight on my left foot.

I have to sit straight back down.

"Where does it hurt?" says Roseanne.

"My ankle. I think it's broken."

"Take your boot off and let's have a look," she says.

I undo my shoelaces and slip my sock off.

"Yeah, it's pretty swollen," she says. "But it's not broken. You're going to need a bandage, though. I've got one in my pack."

Roseanne climbs back up the bank, grabs her first-aid kit, and is back in a flash.

She puts a cream-colored bandage on the top of my foot and wraps it around twice. Then she winds it around my ankle and back under and over my foot again, in a figure-eight motion.

"Where did you learn to do that?" I ask.

"I'm doing my scout training," she informs me matter-of-factly.

"I didn't know that," I say.

"You didn't ask."

At last the others catch up.

"What's going on?" asks Derek, craning his neck to see what we're doing. "You two playing footsy?"

Help. They've just come out my mouth.

"He's hurt his ankle," says Roseanne. "Pretty bad, too."

"Can he walk?" asks Derek.

"Not well," she says. "But he can lean on me. He won't be able to carry his pack, though. We'll have to unpack it and share the load."

Lean on her? Is she crazy? I can't believe what I'm hearing.

Trapdoor
Spider Hole

"It's okay," I say. "I'll be right."

But Roseanne's not listening.

She's lugged my backpack up to the trail and is distributing its contents among the other hikers.

"Hey," she says. "What are you carrying these for?"

Step 1.
Step 2. Rub salt into wound.

She's holding up three rocks, each the size of a small coconut.

I don't believe it.

I can't believe it.

I won't believe it.

Could Danny be that stupid?

This calls for some quick thinking. I don't want to end up looking like an idiot in front of the whole group.

Get back where you belong!

65

A GUIDE TO TRACKS IN THE WOODS

1. DOG

2. Something furry?

3. Gold Fish?

4. Buddhist

5. Merchant Banker

6. Philosopher.

7. Wombat on a bike

8. Porcupine on its back.

"I can explain," I say, trying to act like it's the most normal thing in the world to carry rocks in your pack. "See, I'm a rock collector and . . ."

But Roseanne is shaking her head.

"Why put the rocks in your pack?" she says. "Why not carry them in your head with the rest of the collection?"

Everybody starts laughing. Everybody, that is, except me. And Danny. This is all his fault. I should never have trusted him.

If only he had never had the stupid idea of putting rocks in her pack in the first place!

After Roseanne finishes distributing the contents of my pack, she slides back down the bank.

"Put your arm around my neck," she says. "I'll help you up."

My arm? *Her* neck? She's got to be kidding.

"No, it's okay, thanks," I say. "I think I can walk now."

"Suit yourself," she says.

I grab a small tree and start to pull myself up the bank. But the pain in my ankle is too

66

It's growing back.

much. I miss my footing and fall backward.

Roseanne lifts me up, places my arm over her shoulder, and helps me up the bank.

She might be a pain, but I've got to hand it to her: She knows how to handle an emergency.

Danny is standing at the side of the trail, looking sheepish.

"Maggot-brained moron!" I hiss at him.

He just shrugs. He knows it's the truth.

As I limp alongside Roseanne, we talk. She tells me that this is the sixth school she's been to.

"You got kicked out of five schools?" I ask.

"I wasn't kicked out," she says. "We keep moving. Dad's a structural engineer. He has to keep moving to where the work is. We never stay in one place for more than a year or two."

"Isn't that hard?" I ask.

"A bit," she says. "It's kind of lonely."

After a long afternoon, we've finally made

it to Waterloo Bay. Roseanne hasn't stopped talking and cracking jokes the whole way. Some of them are almost funny, too.

We're the last ones in. I stagger onto the beach and into the camping area behind the sand dunes.

"There you go," says Roseanne. "How's your ankle feeling?"

"A little better."

"Think you'll be right for tomorrow?"

"I hope so," I say.

"Well, if not, give me a yell."

You know, I hate to admit it but, even with all her stupid practical jokes and wisecracks, Roseanne's not so bad. In fact, to tell the truth, I'm kind of starting to like her.

"Thanks, Roseanne. I owe you one."

"You don't owe me anything," she says, putting her hand on my shoulder. "But could you just do me one small favor?"

"What's that?" I say.

She gives me this big cheesy grin and winks.

"Tell yer mom I saved ya!"

BEACH-
COMBERS
GUIDE To
SHELLS

SHELL

BIGGER
SHELL

TWISTED
SHELL

BOTTLECAP
SHELL

Recycle
SHELL

WEIRD!!

THONG FISH

MORE
WOMBAT
ROCKS

what..?

68

Emergency spew relish

t's the last week of school vacation, and I'm flying to Mildura to visit my grand-parents.

I'm on one of those little thirty-six–seater planes.

I've got a window seat, but I want the seat next to me as well. I want to spread out and get comfortable.

I don't think anybody's going to sit there now, but I've laid a piece of rubber dog pooh on the seat, just to make sure.

I'm doing really well. It's almost time for takeoff and nobody's sat there yet, and there are still two empty seats behind me.

An old lady boards the plane and shuffles down the aisle.

With a bit of luck, she'll take the seat behind me and then the flight attendant will close the door and I can relax.

But the old lady stops right next to me. I can't believe it.

No! No! No! I'm thinking. *Keep going!*

"Excuse me," she says, "is this seat taken?"

"Um, er, no, not exactly," I say. "But I don't think I'd sit in it if I were you. . . . It's not very clean."

Rubber dogs don't do poo.

The old lady bends over and pats the seat. She finds the dog pooh, picks it up, and strokes it.

MEN ONLY! The best PRACTICAL JOKE EVER has been moved to keep it from the prying eyes of uninitiated females. GO TO Pg. 9 (nine) NOW!

"It's only a piece of rubber dog pooh," she says. "I suppose it's some young person's idea of a joke."

She puts the pooh into an airsickness bag hanging in front of the seat.

Pretty cool old lady. But how did she know it was only rubber? That's the very best quality rubber dog pooh money can buy. That stuff even fools my dog.

"So I can sit here, after all," she says. "You don't mind, do you?"

I want to say, "Yes, actually. I do mind! There are plenty of empty seats! Why don't you go and sit in one of them?"

But I don't want to be rude, especially not to an old lady. And I can't just get up and go sit in one of the empty seats myself, because she might think I'm being nasty. She might be really lonely and not have any friends, and me going to another seat might be the last straw.

It's going to have to be her who moves.

She puts her handbag underneath her seat and settles in.

This is going to require some pretty quick thinking.

At last the doors are shut and the flight attendant welcomes us on board. She points out the emergency exits, life jackets, and oxygen masks. Some welcome, but it does give me an idea.

The engines start up and fill the plane with their low vibrations.

"I hope it's not too rough a ride," I say, "because I'm a hopeless air traveler. I practically get sick even thinking about planes."

"What?" she says. "You'll have to speak up!"

I lean close to her old wrinkled ear.

"I said, I'm a hopeless air traveler! I always get sick on planes."

The old lady smiles.

"That's good then," she says. "We can look after each other. I'm not much for air travel either!"

Oh great. Just lovely. Not only does she take up my seat, now she's threatening to get sick all over me as well.

The plane shudders and moves forward with a groan.

Takeoff is my favorite part.

The pilot's voice comes over the speakers: "Good morning and thank you for flying with Southern Australia Airlines. We have almost perfect conditions for our flight to Mildura this morning. We'll be cruising at around sixteen thousand feet, at a speed of three hundred miles per hour. We have a

72

slight tail wind, and we expect to reach our destination in just under an hour. We hope you have a pleasant flight."

"What did he say?" says the lady. "What did he say?"

"He said it's going to be pretty rough," I tell her. "Hurricanes and tornadoes are expected. He said to hold tight and just hope and pray that you're not sitting next to someone who's prone to airsickness. He said that it's okay if you want to change seats when the plane stops climbing in a few minutes."

"Well, I'm not going to change seats," says the lady. "I am thankful to be sitting next to a big, strong young man like you. I'd be too scared to sit by myself in conditions like these."

The plane finishes its long slow taxi out to the runway. It turns and then starts rushing forward. I can feel my body being drawn back hard against the seat as the wheels leave the tarmac and we climb steeply into the sky.

The pilot is right, of course. It's one of the smoothest takeoffs ever. But I jiggle and shake and rattle the seats to make it seem really wild and rough.

"Ooohhh," I groan. "Oooooohhhhh. I feel sick already. Are you sure you don't want to change seats?"

"No, love," she says, taking my hand in hers. "I'll look after you."

Oh no! What did I do to deserve this? Now she wants to be my mom!

This calls for serious evasive action.

Forget the emergency life jackets and the emergency oxygen masks. They are absolutely no use to me.

This situation calls for the emergency corn relish.

Actually, I don't call corn relish "corn relish." I call it "spew relish." Because as far as I'm concerned, the only difference between corn relish and spew is that corn relish comes in a jar.

It looks like spew.

It smells like spew.

It even tastes like spew.

The only thing more like spew than corn relish is custard, and I don't even

from piranha to Porsche!

want to think about that because it will
really make me spew.

Anyway, I always carry a jar of spew
relish with me for emergencies just like this.

I slide my hand out of the old lady's.

"It's okay now, thank you," I say. "I'm
feeling much better all of a sudden."

"Well, you just let me know if there's
anything I can do for you," she says.

The flight attendant unbuckles herself
from her seat and starts her mad rush to
offer us all drinks and food. The flight usually
only lasts about an hour. As soon as she's
finished giving out tea, coffee, fruit juices,
cans of soda and bags of pretzels, it'll be
time to collect all the leftovers, pack everything up, and strap herself back into her
seat, ready for touchdown.

...tea,
coffee,
barf
bag?

She approaches our seat.

The old lady orders a cup of tea and
cookies. I want to order one of everything, but
I can't. For the old spew relish trick to work,
I've got to convince her that I'm too sick to eat.

"Nothing for me," I say to the flight
attendant. "Maybe just a little water."

what's that
trailer doing
there?

The flight attendant returns with the tea. While the old lady's busy adding her sugar and milk, I reach down to my bag and dig out my jar of spew relish.

By the time I'm through, this old lady is not going to want to sit next to me.

She's not going to even want to sit on the same plane as me.

In fact, I'll make sure she never even wants to *go* on a plane again.

I'm bent over, facing the wall of the plane so the old lady can't see what I'm doing. I screw the lid off the jar. I pinch my nose and tip the jar of spew relish up to my mouth. I try to suck in as much as I can without swallowing. I manage to get about half the jar in. Lucky I've got such a big mouth.

I put the lid back on the jar and tuck it back into my bag.

I sit back in my seat, hold my belly, and moan quietly.

"Are you all right?" says the old lady.

I can't answer, of course, because my mouth's full.

I just groan, louder this time.

76

I don't like the look of this.

"Do you need a sick bag?" she says.

I nod.

She grabs a bag from in front of her — the one with my rubber dog pooh in it — and passes it to me.

I rock back and forth and puff out my cheeks and then pretend to splurk up into the bag. Not that it all goes into the bag, of course.

I take care to dribble some down my chin and onto my T-shirt.

"Oh, you poor thing," says the old lady. "You poor old thing."

Huh? *She's* calling *me* old?

"I'm okay now, thanks," I say. "That feels much better."

"You know, it's funny," she says, "but I'm not feeling sick at all. This is one of the smoothest flights I've ever had. You must have a very delicate stomach."

"Extremely delicate," I say. "But I'm really hungry now."

"Oh, what a pity," she says. "You're too late to order anything."

"That's okay," I say. "I brought my own. Could I borrow your teaspoon?"

AMAZING
EYE
TRICK#3
ANSWER
If you have done this amazing trick correctly, you should now be looking at the back of my living room. AMAZING!

May I borrow your hand b2q?

TA.

77
Oh, oh!

"Why certainly," she says. "Here you are."

I take the teaspoon. This is it. Any minute now she'll be out of her seat like a rocket.

"Well, down the hatch."

I open the neck of the sick bag and dip the spoon in. I scoop up a spoonful of spew relish and pull it out of the bag. I pass the spoon under my nose a couple of times and sniff deeply.

"Ahhh!" I say, smiling. "I love it when it's nice and warm and fresh!"

I open my mouth very slowly. I put the teaspoon on my tongue and close my mouth. Then I slowly draw the teaspoon out and lick it clean, making sure I get every last drop. I close my eyes and sigh, as if I'm in heaven.

I open my eyes. I expect to see the seat next to me empty. I expect the old lady to be as far away from me as possible, and warning everybody else to stay away, too.

But the seat is not empty.

The old lady is still there. Still watching.

"Was that nice?" she asks.

"It was beautiful," I say. "Tasted even better going down than it did coming up."

JUMBO BUNGEE. ?

78

"That's nice," she says. "I'm glad. Have some more."

What?

If she'd said, "Let's take our clothes off and run up and down the aisle," I would have been only half as surprised.

"Um, okay, thanks. I will."

I eat another spoonful. Only this time I finish with a big belch.

"Excuse me," I say.

"Oh, don't mention it," says the old lady. "In some countries, it's good manners to burp after a meal. It's considered a compliment to the cook."

This old lady is unshakable. If she thinks this is normal, I'd hate to see mealtimes at her house.

This calls for some serious grossing-outing.

I get another spoonful and, instead of putting it in my mouth, I plonk it on top of my head.

"Makes great shampoo, too," I say. "Or should I say 'sham-spew'?"

The old lady just nods.

I load up my spoon again, and this time I splatter spew relish all over my face. I rub it into my eyes, my cheeks, my ears.

"I reckon it's just a great all-round beauty cream," I say. "Do you find that gross?"

The old lady just looks on, a slight smile on her face.

"No," she says calmly. "In fact, I'd love to try some of this amazing food that doubles as a beauty cream. What do you call it?"

That's when it hits me.

I hold up three fingers in front of her face.

"How many fingers am I holding up?" I ask her.

She pauses.

"I don't know, dear. I'm blind. Why do you ask?"

"No reason," I say, trying not to gag from the stench of the spew relish, which I just know I'm not going to be able to get out of my skin and hair for months. "No reason at all. But I think I'm going to be sick again."

"Oh, you poor thing," says the old lady, passing me another sick bag. "You poor old thing."

BEAT THE BOMB!

anny and I are about to play the most wicked joke in history. We've been working on it all morning. We owe the idea to my mom.

Mom listens to the radio nonstop. It's always on in the kitchen. Wouldn't be so bad if she listened to something good, like Triple J, but she prefers the golden-oldie station Triple B. The B stands for Boredom. Talk about sad music. It's so sad and boring, they have to run competitions all the time to bribe people to listen to it.

They've got this competition at the moment called Beat the Bomb. Every hour they call up a listener and then start the clock ticking. Every few seconds, over the sound of the clock, a voice says ever-increasing amounts of money, like "One hundred dollars... one hundred and fifty-five dollars... two hundred and three dollars..." and so on. The listener has to tell the DJ when to stop, and if they do it before the bomb explodes, then they get to keep that amount of money. It can last anywhere from a couple of seconds to half a minute.

The trick is having the nerve to let the clock tick for as long as possible. I've never heard anyone win more than a few hundred dollars, but still, that'd buy a lot of CDs, a heap of chocolate, and a lot of video games at the arcade.

All you have to do to be in it is send a letter with your name and telephone number to Triple B. If they draw yours from the barrel, they call you and you get a chance to play.

I've sent in about fifteen letters. I figure that makes me fifteen times more likely to win. I don't think anybody else would be

BLAH BLAH BLAH

clever enough to have thought of that.

But in the meantime, while I wait for them to call, Danny and I are going to have some fun. We've recorded the station signature tune, a couple of advertisements, and a couple of songs. And I can do a pretty convincing imitation of a DJ when I try. We're going to ring Marvin Bonwick and pretend that he's about to play Beat the Bomb.

Why Marvin Bonwick? Because we always play jokes on Marvin Bonwick. He takes everything so seriously. We use his name whenever we get the chance. Like writing comments on the service evaluation cards at KFC. We always write dumb things like: This KFC stinks. I wanted fish, but the cashier wouldn't give me any. She said you've got nothing but chicken. That sucks! Yours sincerely, Marvin Bonwick. P.S. What does KFC stand for anyway?

We always supply his full name, address, and phone number. I'd give anything to hear what they say when they call him up to discuss his comments.

"Let's do it," says Danny. "It's ten past four."

"Okay," I say. I pick up the receiver and start dialing.

Danny is laughing.

"Hey, shut up," I say. "It's ringing!"

"Hello?"

It's a woman speaking. Must be his mother.

"Hello — it's Chris Robbins from Triple B FM," I say in my radio voice. "Could I speak to Marvin Bonwick please?"

"Yes, just a minute. Marvin!" she calls. "Telephone! He'll be with you in a minute," she says. "Marvin!"

Knowing Marvin, he's probably doing homework.

Finally he picks up the phone.

"Hello?"

"Marvin Bonwick?"

"Yes."

"Chris Robbins from Triple B FM here. How are you doing?"

"Good . . . What did you say your name was?"

"Chris Robbins. Your name's been drawn this hour to play Beat the Bomb."

"Beat the what?"

84

...and some grilled flake.

DUE TO UNFORSEEN CIRCUMSTANCES the best practical joke ever is now on:
1. Female Version Pg.111.
2. Male Version Pg. 125.

"Beat the Bomb!"

"What's that?"

"You know, our competition. You should know — you entered it. I've got a letter here with your name on it."

"I don't remember doing that."

"Well, maybe a friend did it for you. Would you like to have a try?"

"Sure," he says.

"Well, stand by, we're about to go to air. I'll just play a couple of ads and a station ID, and then you're on. Oh, and by the way, Marvin?"

"Yes?"

"Turn your radio off. We will be transmitting on a ten-second delay, and it can get very confusing."

I point at Danny. He presses the tape-recorder. It starts into a jingle for Cheapies carpet-cleaning service. I put the phone right next to the speaker.

"I think we've got him!" I whisper to Danny.

The carpet ad finishes and one for a supermarket starts. Then the Triple B station ID comes on. It sounds really spacey, like

This book is printed on paper made from 100% Dolphin Skin (Recycled).

PARTS OF THE BODY # 121

The finger. (Really a crocodile pretending)

I'm bored.

comets and meteorites whizzing past your ears.

"Triple B — taking you back to the sixties and seventies..." says the voice-over. The sound of the meteorites ends in a shower of xylophone notes. It's the only exciting sound on the whole station.

"Good afternoon," I say. "Chris Robbins with you on Triple B, and to play Beat the Bomb this hour we have Marvin Bonwick on the line. How are you doin,' Marvy?"

"Good."

"Great! What are you up to this afternoon?"

"Nothing much, you know."

"Fantastic! Ready to play?"

"Yes."

"All right — now, you know the rules, Marvy?"

"No," he says.

"I'm going to start the clock ticking. You say stop when you think you've won enough, and it's yours to keep. But don't let it go on too long. If the bomb explodes, you end up empty-handed!"

AMAZING
EYE
TRICKS #4:

Stare at
the space
between
these shapes.

Does it
remind
you of
anything?
Ans: Pg 102

86

my impression
of a double
ended fish.

"Yeah, no problem."

"Okay. Clock's ticking."

Danny switches tapes and presses play.

Tick tick tick tick tick tick tick

He picks up an empty cardboard tube and puts one end to the telephone and the other to his mouth.

"Twenty dollars," he says. The tube gives his voice the spacey echo of the real voice. It's the sort of attention to detail that makes our practical jokes so special.

Tick tick tick tick tick tick tick

Marvin says nothing.

"One hundred and sixty-three dollars," says Danny, obviously enjoying himself.

"Three hundred and fifteen dollars."

Silence. This guy's got nerves of steel. Either that or he's really greedy. Most people would have bailed out by now.

"Three hundred and eighty-three dollars."

Danny looks at me. I shrug.

"Four hundred and forty-four dollars!" says Danny.

Tick tick tick tick tick tick tick

"Five hundred dollars."

87
A hammerhead shark

"Stop!" says Marvin.

I signal to Danny to stop the tape.

"Marvin?"

"Yes?"

"Do you know what you've just done?"

"No, did I do something wrong?"

"Wrong? Marvin, you have just won five hundred dollars! What do you think about that?"

Are you UGLY. Now Dr. Griffith's Corrective Surgery can end your embarrassment.

TRY THIS,
↓

OR THIS,
↓

OR THIS.
↓

"That's fantastic! I can't believe it! Mom — I just won five hundred dollars!"

Marvin's mother starts squealing in the background. She's so loud, I have to hold the receiver away from my ear. Danny can hear it, too. He's rolling around on the floor, killing himself laughing.

"Hey, Marvy," I say. "What are you going to do with all that money?"

"I don't know," says Marvin. "I don't know. I've never won anything like this!"

"Well congratulations, Marvy. Now, if you can stay on the line while we get some details, Elton John is going to take us back and show us how to do the Crocodile Rock. This is Triple B FM where — like Marvin

A parrot fish.

Bonwick — we make your dreams come true. Well done, Marvy!"

"Thanks, mate!" he says.

Danny starts playing "Crocodile Rock."

We're about to yell, "Just kidding, you stupid jerk!" when I hear a strange sound on the other end of the line. Like somebody crying.

I can hear Marvin talking.

"It's okay, Mom, it's okay. You should be happy!"

"I am happy," she says.

Why would she be crying?

Danny's laughing so hard I'm worried he's going to wet himself.

"Shhh!" I tell him. "Shut up!"

"What's wrong?" he says.

"I'm not sure," I tell him. "Just keep the noise down."

Danny screws up his face.

"Marvy, are you still there?" I say.

"Yeah, sorry, Mom's a bit emotional."

"That's understandable," I say. "Five hundred dollars is a lot of money."

"Yeah," says Marvin. "Especially for us.

89
(A flathead.)

KICK ME

See, since Dad died, we've been really struggling. Mom has to work pretty long hours to hold things together. This money is really going to help out. You've got no idea how much it means to us."

Are you waiting to see the SCHOOL PRINCIPAL?

As Marvin talks, I feel smaller and smaller. How was I to know his dad died? He didn't say anything. Not that he would have told me — I don't know him that well. But someone could have said something.

Then, try eating his indoor plants to stumps. He'll be very impressed

"Yeah, ah, um, glad to be able to help out, Marvy. Now if I could just get your address . . ."

Well, what else can I say? Somehow, "Just kidding, you stupid jerk" doesn't seem quite as witty as it did a few minutes ago.

Danny's stopped laughing. He's frowning and looking at me like I'm crazy.

"What?" he says.

I wave him away with my hand.

I take down Marvin's address.

"Thanks, Marvy. We'll send you a letter in the next few days with details of how to collect your money."

"Chris," says Marvy, "can I just say that

I'm still bored

you've made me and my mom really happy today. Thanks a lot."

"Don't mention it," I say, and hang up.

"Are you out of your mind?" says Danny.

"His dad died."

"So?"

"They really need the money."

"So you promised it to them?"

I nod.

"Oh, man . . ." Danny is shaking his head.

"His mom was crying, Dan. He said they've been really struggling. I couldn't tell them it was just a joke. I couldn't."

"So, you're going to send him five hundred dollars because you feel bad about a little practical joke."

"It's not a *little* practical joke," I say. "It is an almighty mess-up."

"Know what I think?" says Danny.

"What?"

"Just do nothing. That way there's no need to explain. There's nothing to trace it back to us."

"But what if they call the radio station?"

Don't turn this next page or I'll explode.

"The radio station won't know anything about it," says Danny. "Marvin will realize it was a joke."

"But that's terrible!" I say. "Think how he'll feel. That's even worse than admitting it was a hoax. After all they've been through! No — we've got to get them that money."

"What do you propose? Rob a bank?"

"No. We'll wash cars, mow lawns, pool all our allowance — and then we'll invest it in a high-interest bank account. We'll have the money in no time."

"We?" says Danny.

"What do you mean?"

"*You* made the call."

"You helped me."

"But it was your idea."

"You didn't say no."

Danny hits himself on the head with his open palm. "Do you have any idea how many cars we'll have to wash to earn that much money?!"

The phone rings.

I pick it up.

"Hello."

"Hi, could I speak to Andy Griffiths?"

"Speaking."

"Hi, Andy. Chris Robbins from Triple B FM here."

My stomach drops. He must have found out I've been impersonating him! Marvin Bonwick must have rung him back to check if the call was legit! When he found out it was a trick, he would have guessed it was me.

"Who is it?" says Danny.

I put my hand over the receiver. "It's Chris Robbins! He must know! What do I do?"

"Talk to him," says Danny. "He can't prove anything."

"Andy?" says Chris. "Are you still there?"

"Yes," I say. "I'm here."

"Thought we'd lost you for a minute."

"Just a bit surprised," I say. "What can I do for you?"

"Well," says Chris, "I've just pulled your name out of the barrel to play Beat the Bomb — but if you'd rather not . . ."

"Are you kidding?" I shout. "Of course I want to!"

It's like a dream. What are the odds of

Don't turn the page ... or I'll turn into an electrical appliance.

93

KICK ME

something like this happening? A million to one? Nah — more like a squillion to one.

"Well, stand by," says Chris. "We're about to go to air. I'll just play a couple of ads and a station ID and then you're on. Oh, and by the way, Andy?"

"Yes?"

"Turn your radio off. We will be transmitting on a ten-second delay and it can get a little confusing."

Through the earpiece of the telephone, I hear a jingle for Cheapies carpet-cleaning service. Talk about déjà vu. If Danny wasn't right next to me, I'd swear it was him playing another prank.

Then the Triple B station ID starts. Comets and meteorites again. "Triple B — taking you back to the sixties and seventies . . ."

Then Chris starts speaking.

"Good afternoon. Chris Robbins with you on Triple B, and to play Beat the Bomb this hour, we have Andy Griffiths on the line. How are you doin', Andy?"

"Pretty good."

BIG TOE,
with trapdoor
to allow
toe bone
to get
some
air
every now
and
then.

"Great! What are you up to this afternoon?"

I wonder what he would say if I told him I was impersonating him and making prank Beat the Bomb phone calls. But I decide against it. I need the cash.

"Nothing much, you know."

"Fantastic! Ready to play Beat the Bomb?"

"I sure am."

"All right — now, you know the rules, Andy?"

"Yes," I say, but he explains them anyway.

"Okay. Clock's ticking," says Chris.

"Twenty dollars," says the voice from outer space.

Tick tick tick tick tick tick tick

I'd be happy with twenty. Maybe I should stop it right now. Those bombs can go off pretty fast sometimes.

"Twenty-five dollars."

Tick tick tick tick tick tick tick

"One hundred and forty-eight dollars."

I want to stop, but I can't. It's like I'm frozen. If I can just keep my nerve . . .

"Two hundred and ninety dollars."

Tick tick tick tick tick tick tick

HEALTH
TIP.
If your
brain
starts
leaking
out of
your
ear,

place
an old
cork
in your
earhole
and
hammer
it in.

Your
toast's
ready.

95

KICK
ME

"Four hundred and sixty-six dollars."

The ticking is deafening. Any minute now, the bomb is going to explode, and I'll be splattered all over the room. But still I can't speak.

"Five hundred and two dollars."

I can't stand it anymore.

"Stop!" I yell.

"Andy?"

"Yes?"

"Do you know what you've just done?"

"Yes," I say in a dream.

"You have just won five hundred and two dollars! What do you think about that?"

I can't speak.

Danny's jumping up and down.

"How much?" he's asking. "How much?!"

"Five hundred and two," I say.

Danny hoots.

"Hey, Andy," says Chris. "What are you going to do with all that money?"

A vision of a pile of Mars bars as high as Mount Everest fills my head. It merges into a tower of CDs and a stereo system loud enough to blow my ears off. And then it

An old piece of wood

↓

Ask yourself, "Where has it come from?"

Didn't I ask you not to turn the page?

dissolves into a blinding vision of flashing lights and beeps and explosions as I imagine spending an entire weekend in the arcade. But then I think of Marvin. And his mom.

"I'm not sure," I say. "Maybe I'll give it to a friend."

Danny raises his eyebrows.

"Well, good for you, Andy," says Chris. "Now, if you can stay on the line while we confirm your details, we've got something special coming up. Do you like John Farnham, Andy?"

I can't stand him, but I'll say anything for five hundred and two bucks.

"*Like* him? I *love* him!" I lie.

"Well then, this is for you," he says over the start of "You're the Voice." "This is Triple B FM where, like Andy Griffiths, we make your dreams, and your friends' dreams, come true. Good for you, Andy!"

"Thanks," I say.

My head is spinning. I'm trying to work out if I'm the most fantastically lucky person or the biggest loser in the world. I mean, having to pretend I like John Farnham is

Don't turn the page or I'll turn into a Septic Tank.

BATTERIES

BATTERY HEN

KICK ME

bad enough, but having one of his songs dedicated to me is much, much worse.

"Are you going to give that money to me?" says Danny. He's practically drooling all over the carpet.

"No," I say. "What makes you think that?"

"You said you were going to give it to a friend."

"Yes, but not you," I say.

"Then who?"

"Marvin."

His jaw drops.

"You're kidding!"

"No," I say.

"All of it?"

"No, not all of it. After I pay Marvin what we owe him, there will be two dollars left over. We can go halves in that if you like."

"Thanks," says Danny, staring at the carpet. "You're a real pal."

"Don't mention it," I say. "What are friends for?"

So you think a cockroach has an I.Q. of 120, eh? That'd make me twice as smart as you. Try again.

Wow!! I've been run over by a HONDA 750cc...

HA. HA. HA Tricked You!!

Born to Die

Well, I finally did it.

I've been thinking about it for ages and I kept putting it off, but this morning I finally did it.

I got a tattoo.

It's a skull with two eagle wings curving up over the top. The skull has these evil green eyes and a sort of long, thin red mustache that arches upward next to the wings. And running across the bottom of the skull is a small ribbon-shaped banner. And inside the banner are the words BORN TO DIE.

Didn't cost much either. Normally, it would have cost two dollars and ninety-five cents, but I got it on special at Target for ninety-nine cents.

And the best thing about it is that it didn't even hurt.

I just removed the protective sheet and pressed the sticky side firmly onto my skin. Then I wet the top of it with a sponge, waited for thirty seconds, and peeled off the backing.

Yeah, so it's not real — but it's so realistic you'd never know the difference. And the amazing thing is, it makes me feel different. Bigger. Tougher. Bolder. Nobody's going to want to kick sand in my face and steal my girlfriend when they see I've got such an awesome tat. Not that I have a girlfriend right at the moment, but as soon as they see my tattoo, I bet every girl in school will want to go out with me — even the teachers.

The package says it will last for days — almost forever. It also says I'll be able to shock my friends and family. But it's not my friends and family I'm interested in shocking. It's my enemies: Steve Lik and Robert Leech.

Steve Lik lives at the bottom of the hill.

100

oh look, a nice worm.

He's a few years older than me, but we used to hang out together on weekends. Until he started hanging around with Robert Leech.

Robert Leech is a wiry-haired geek who lives over on the other side of the hill.

He's got a face like a rat, with a really thin pointy nose and beady brown eyes. He thinks he's really cool because he rides a fifteen-speed racer and smokes. He doesn't like me much. Well, to be truthful, he hates my guts. I don't know what I did to make him hate me so much. Being born I suppose. Robert Leech is just that sort of guy.

I hate your guts.

Lately, him and Lik have taken to waiting for me at the bottom of the hill outside Lik's place, and they won't let me pass until I tell them the password. Today is no exception. I turn the corner into my street and they're both there, like they've been waiting for me. Leech is sitting in the middle of the side-walk. He's got his jaws rigid and his lips tight as he blows a series of smoke rings. Lik is leaning against his mailbox with a yellow

How to impress your school principal.

Wrap masking tape around your face and pretend to be his mummy.

101

I think I'll eat it.

bucket in his hand. I could try crossing the road, but I know they'd just come after me. I pretend to ignore them.

"Well, well, well," says Leech, in between smoke rings. "If it isn't our old friend, Andy."

Lik smirks.

"Do you mind if I just go past?" I say, moving to step around him. But Leech's hand shoots out and grabs my ankle.

"Not so fast," he says. "Say please."

"Please," I say, looking straight ahead.

"Say pretty please," he says. "With sugar on top."

"Pretty please with sugar on top," I say.

"Say pretty please with sugar on top, sir!"

I know from experience that this can go on for a long time. But today I don't have to put up with this crap because I've got a tattoo. I casually roll up the sleeves of my windbreaker. The tattoo is still there on my right forearm. The skull's eyes seem to be flashing.

"Look, I don't want any trouble," I say. "Just let me past . . . or else."

Leech laugh. "Or else what?" He is too busy blowing smoke rings to notice my

AMAZING EYE TRICK #2 ANSWER

Have you forgotten? You promised your mom you'd take the laundry off the line. And it's been raining.!! You're in trouble.

102

You could warn me.

tattoo. But I can see that Lik has seen it. He's already backing off.

"Come on, Leechy. That'll do."

Leech stops laughing. "Huh?"

Lik steps across to him and whispers in his ear.

Leech jumps up from the sidewalk, his eyes fixed on my forearm. He takes a couple of steps backward.

"Can I pass now?" I ask.

"Yeah, of c-course," says Leech. "We were just kidding around. Just a little fun, you know."

"Fun? That's what you call fun?"

Leech and Lik are standing there frozen, like a couple of stunned rabbits. I'm not sure whether they're scared of the tattoo or just the way it makes me act, but I don't really care. I flex the muscles in my forearm, which is a hard thing to do really, because I don't have that many. But my skull doesn't mind. It ripples and seems to grin in response, like it's enjoying it. I guess I should be scared, but I feel strangely calm. Like I can do whatever I want. Why not pull out all the stops and teach them a lesson they'll never forget?

You know perfectly well there's a hook there.

If you turn this page, your undies will fall down, your nose will drop off, and all your hair will fall out. And you will start barking like a dog.

Lik is still holding the yellow bucket.

"What's in the bucket?" I say.

"Slugs," says Lik.

"How come?" I ask, knowing full well that they get their kicks out of inventing new and horrible ways for slugs to die.

"Um, er, well, my dad asked me to. They've been eating his rose bushes."

"Don't give me that," I say. "Let 'em go."

Lik looks at Leech. Leech nods. Lik tips the bucket, and about twenty fat gray slugs fall into the shrubbery.

I watch them helplessly trying to untangle themselves from one another and shake my head.

"You know," I say, "maybe it's just me, but I don't find that very funny."

Lik and Leech are both silent.

"And another thing I don't find very funny is you two hassling me every time I walk past. It's got to stop."

"Sorry," says Lik. "We were just messing around. How about a milk shake to make up for it?"

I should leave here and just keep walking

104

I could be caught

SEE,
We
warned
you!!

up the hill, but I'm enjoying my newfound power too much. I remember the cool milk shakes that Lik use to make for me back in the days when we were friends. Two heaped teaspoons of malt, eggs, ice cream, and about half a bottle of chocolate syrup.

"Thought you'd never ask," I say.

"Okay," says Lik. "I'll go get you one, won't be a sec."

skeleton
staff
↓

"No, not takeout," I say. "I think I'll drink it inside, if that's okay with you. Sun's kind of hot today."

Leech and Lik look at each other.

"Yeah, Andy," says Lik. "Of course. Come in."

We start walking up the driveway. I'm so cool I can't believe it.

Inside, I pick the best seat in the living room and plonk my feet up on the coffee table. There's a pile of magazines on top of the table, so I push them all off to the carpet with my feet.

"I think I'll just wait here while you make my milk shake," I say.

"Sure, fine," says Lik.

105
Dragged out
of the water

I grab the remote and turn on the television. I turn up the sound full blast so that it's distorted.

Lik pokes his head around the door.

"Hey, Andy!" he says.

"What?"

"Can you turn that down a little?"

"No," I say. "I like it loud."

Good night Frank. See you same time next week.

Lik just stands there like he's not sure whether to rip the remote out of my hand and shove it down my throat or just leave it.

"Wanna make something of it?" I say.

"No," he says, "of course not. You're the guest. What flavor milk shake do you want?"

"Chocolate, of course," I say.

"Coming right up," he says and goes back into the kitchen.

I start flipping through the channels on the remote. *Playschool* on Channel Two. The hosts are pretending to be kookaburras. They're singing a song.

Kookaburra sits on the old gum tree,
merry merry king of the bush is he: . . .

I know exactly how that kookaburra feels. I'm the king and Lik and Leech are my

Beaten to death with a bit of wood.

subjects. They will do anything I tell them to. I watch a bit more of *Playschool,* then turn it off.

"What's taking so long?" I call.

"Almost ready," yells Leech.

I hear the high-pitched whine of the blender. My mouth starts watering. Steve Lik's milk shakes are really something else.

The blender stops.

"I don't want it in the container either," I say. "I want it in a glass. With a straw!"

"No problem," calls Lik.

Leech enters the room with the milk shake on a tray. Lik is right behind him.

Leech places the tray on top of the coffee table. The milk shake is in one of those old-fashioned glasses with ridges down the side and a crazy straw sticking out. There is a scoop of chocolate ice cream sitting on top.

Lik picks up the glass and gives it to me. Then they both kneel down on either side of my chair and stare at me.

"Do you mind?" I say.

"No," says Leech, his lips curling into a slight smile.

SIMPSON and his Porcupine.

A really tough guy

107

Scaled, filleHed, cooked, and eaten.

"Well, what are you waiting for?"

"We just want to watch you drink it," says Lik.

Tough guys eat petals...

Bicycle pedals!

"We just want to watch you *enjoy* it," says Leech.

There's something about the way he says "enjoy" that I don't like.

I push my arm forward to make sure they remember who's boss here. I look at them, look at my tattoo and look back at them to make sure they've got the message.

But they just start laughing. My stomach drops.

"Would you mind sharing the joke with me?" I say.

"Should we?" says Lik.

"Yes," says Leech. "I think we should."

Leech pulls up his sleeve. Lik pulls up his sleeve.

On each of their arms, in almost exactly the same place as mine, is a skull with green eyes and a long red mustache.

I look at them.

They look at me.

The room is very quiet.

Then who'd tell you what page number it is?

"Well, drink up," says Lik. "We're waiting."

"Um," I say, "look, thanks for the milk shake and everything, but I'm not really that thirsty. I might just get going."

I sit forward to get up, but Lik pushes me back into my seat.

"After we've gone to all this trouble? Surely you've got a minute just to drink a milk shake. You can't waste it."

"Okay," I say. "But then I've really got to get going."

"Sure," says Lik. "Drink up."

I guess there are worse punishments.

I put the glass to my lips.

"Oh, there's just one thing," says Leech. "Hope you don't mind, but we couldn't find any chocolate syrup."

I'm starting to sweat.

"That's okay," I say, trying to keep cool. "What did you use instead?"

"Slugs," says Leech. "Now drink up."

WANTING
FOR THE
PRINCIPAL?
Charm
him by
swallowing
all the
School
Goldfish.

GULP!

invisipills

Mrs. Wharton is stomping around the library. She's telling kids off for talking. She's telling kids off for leaning back on their chairs. She's practically telling kids off for breathing. You name it, and she's telling them off for it.

I reckon she's wasted as a librarian. Mrs. Wharton should have been the warden of a high-security prison. That'd be one prison where they wouldn't have to worry about the prisoners talking, leaning back on their chairs, or returning their library books late.

The only person Mrs. Wharton has not told off so far is me. That's because I'm working so hard. It's pretty rare for me to work this hard, but I have a big assignment on Antarctic explorers due on Monday. It's worth fifty percent of our final grade, and I've only just started it.

The trouble is, Danny is sitting at the desk next to mine and he keeps going on and on about how he wants to be invisible. He won't shut up. He's been talking about it for weeks now. Normally, I wouldn't mind, but I don't want to risk getting kicked out of the library because I need to use the Internet.

"Psst! Andy!" says Danny.

"Shh!" I say to him. "Do you want to get us kicked out?"

"No," he says, "just tell me what you think. If I got a can of spray paint and painted myself pink and painted my whole room pink and everything in it pink, do you think I'd be invisible then?"

"Well, maybe," I whisper. "As long as you stayed in your room. But once you left, you'd be a bit conspicuous."

"Oh," he says.

He's quiet for a few seconds. Then he

leans over again.

"Psst!"

"What!?" I say. I'm getting really impatient.

"What does 'conspicuous' mean?"

"It means you'd stand out like a pimple on a pumpkin! Now would you shut up and do some work — and stop interrupting me!"

"Yeah, sorry," he says. "But honestly, do you think it would work?"

"For the last time, shut up!"

I reach into my pencil case for some candy. Well, they're *supposed* to be candy. They're really just those little multicolored balls with no taste. Nobody likes them except three-year-olds, and that's only because they don't know any better. I'm only eating them because they were a present from my grandma. It would have been rude to throw them away.

I crunch one between my teeth.

Danny leans over.

"What are those?" he says.

Suddenly I have an idea of how to get rid of him.

Mrs. Wharton is up at the counter checking out some books. This gives me a few minutes.

"Danny, what would you say if I had a way of really making you invisible?"

"How?"

I pass him the tube of candy.

"I was waiting until your birthday to give you these, but since you want to be invisible so badly, you might as well have them now."

"What are they?" he says.

"They're invisipills. They make you invisible."

"For real?"

"Absolutely."

"Where'd you get them?" he asks.

"I made them in science. I got the recipe off the Net."

Great Places to HIDE!

Danny hits his head with his hand. "Oh, man! Why didn't I think of that! Which site?"

"I'd rather not say. The recipe was smuggled out of the Pentagon. Top-secret stuff. I could get into a lot of trouble if I'm caught."

"Have you tried them?"

"Yep."

"And?"

I'm the Page № Piranha

113

"They're pretty amazing. One pill will make you completely invisible for about half an hour."

"Wow! How come you didn't tell me?"

"Like I said, I was keeping it for a surprise for your birthday."

"Can I try one?"

"Sure. Just one, though. They're pretty powerful. And you've got to promise me one thing."

"What?" says Danny.

"That after you've taken it, you'll go outside and let me work."

"No problem," he says.

He takes a candy from the tube.

His eyes are wide as he puts it onto his tongue, closes his mouth, and swallows.

"Well?" he says. "Am I invisible?"

"Not yet," I say. "It takes a few minutes."

Danny's holding his hands out in front of him, fingers outstretched.

"Have I faded even a little bit?" he says. "What do you think?"

I screw up my eyes, pretending to study him.

FAMILY JOKE TIME!

Place a live spider under the lid of your mom/dad's deodorant. Guaranteed laughs.

114

"Yes, definitely!" I say. "No doubt about it."

"Cool!" he says.

I glance up. Mrs. Wharton has finished at the counter and is prowling the library again.

"You're fading fast now," I say. "I can hardly see you."

Amazing EYE TRICK N° 5

Which of these two circles is the bigger?

a. O

b. ◯

(Look carefully!) A**N**S: Pg 129

"No I'm not," he says. "I can still see me as clear as anything."

"Yeah — you're supposed to, you dork. That's the way the pills are designed. You can see yourself, but nobody can see you. If you couldn't see yourself, you wouldn't know where you were and you'd get lost."

"Oh, I get it," he says. "So, am I invisible yet?"

Dr. Griffiths' Corrective Surgery

"Where are you?"

"I'm right here!"

"No you're not. Not as far as I can see. Your chair is empty."

"Can you still hear me?"

"Yes. Now go outside! Remember our deal?"

"Okay," says Danny. "I'm outta here."

Danny gets up out of his seat and walks off. Mrs. Wharton is coming slowly toward me. I go back to my assignment and do my

BEFORE

AFTER.

I am!

best imitation of a serious student.

Just as she's walking past my desk, I hear the most enormous belch.

It's so loud it practically rocks the foundations of the library.

For a moment I think it was Mrs. Wharton. But that, of course, is ridiculous. Only Danny can do them that loud.

I look around. Sure enough, Danny is killing himself laughing in the aisle.

Mrs. Wharton stops.

Grezt Places to Hide.

"Excuse me!" she says. "Was that you?"

"No, Mrs. Wharton," I say.

"Then who was it, pray tell? A ghost?"

"I don't know, Mrs. Wharton. But it wasn't me."

"I don't believe you. What are those?" she says, pointing to the candies, which Danny has thoughtfully left sitting on my desk in full view.

"Um . . . candy, Mrs. Wharton."

"I presume you know the rule about eating in the library."

"Yes, Mrs. Wharton."

"And you know that it specifically excludes

I was here first.

chewing gum, bubble gum, *and* candy?"

"Yes, Mrs. Wharton. I'll get rid of them."

"No you won't," she says. "*I* will."

She holds out her hand. I pick up the tube and give it to her. Little does she realize she's doing me a big favor.

She walks up the aisle without another word.

That was close. I'm going to kill Danny after school. With any luck, he's kept his promise and is outside by now.

Thump!

A book lands on the carpet next to my desk. It's *The Wonderful World of Freshwater Fish*, and I have no doubt who threw it.

Another book sails over the top of the shelves and lands on my desk. *Whack!* Another hits the top edge of the desk and bounces off onto the student in front of me.

"Ouch!" he yells, turning to me. "Quit it!"

I shrug.

"It wasn't me," I say.

The books keep coming. And so does Mrs. Wharton.

"Stand up!" she says. "Would you mind

No, I was.

telling me what's going on here?"

"Somebody is throwing books over the tops of the shelves," I say.

Dr. Griffiths' Corrective Surgery.

BEFORE

"Who?"

"I don't know."

She strides off and checks each of the aisles. Any moment now she's going to see Danny and chuck him out. Good riddance, I figure.

AFTER

"I can't see anybody," she says. "Perhaps you'd better tell me how these books really ended up on the floor."

I don't know what to say.

Over Mrs. Wharton's shoulder I can see the A–G fiction shelf rocking back and forth. Danny's gone crazy. The excitement of thinking he's invisible has gone to his head. I've got to stop him before he goes too far.

"Excuse me, Mrs. Wharton," I say. "Back in a minute."

"Where do you think you're going?"

I dash to the seriously rocking shelf to try to pull Danny away and bring him to his senses, but it's already too late. The shelf tilts too far to the right. All the books fall

You're too messy.

onto the carpet. The force of the bookshelf striking the next shelf pushes it over and the combined weight of these two pushes the third shelf over. Just like a row of dominoes. Except heavier. And louder.

There is silence. Nobody can believe what they've just seen.

I turn around. Mrs. Wharton is speechless. She is opening and closing her mouth like a fish.

GREAT PLACES TO HIDE.

But Danny hasn't finished yet.

He's approaching Mrs. Wharton from behind, one of her prized hanging-basket ferns in his hand. The ferns that she waters so lovingly every morning before school. The ferns that if anyone so much as looks at them, let alone touches them, they get one of Mrs. Wharton's famous glares.

Danny's staring straight ahead and carrying the potted plant in his raised outstretched arms, like it's a trophy.

"No!" I yell, but it's like he's possessed.

He tips it upside down over Mrs. Wharton's head. Fern fronds and clumps of dirt and little white fertilizer pellets spill all over her hair, down her face, and onto her yellow dress. They collect in a pile at her feet.

Danny is just standing there laughing. Poor guy. He still thinks he's invisible.

Mrs. Wharton wheels around.

"Just what do you think you're doing?" she says to him.

"Who?" he says.

"You!" she says, going red in the face.

"But you can't see me," says Danny. "I'm invisible!"

WEIRD
PLACES
TO HIDE.

"Invisible? Well, we'll see about that!" she says.

She reaches out, grabs his ear, and twists it at least 360 degrees — and then, judging by the expression on Danny's face, another 360 degrees after that.

Danny drops to his knees in pain.

"Oww! Oww! Let go!" he says.

HUMAN
BODY
PARTS
№ 47B.

The
Tongue

"There," she says. "Feeling a little more visible now?"

I must admit I'm rather enjoying the spectacle. After all, Danny had no qualms about getting me into trouble.

Now you're being silly!

Mrs. Wharton lets go of his ear.

"Now," she says, looking from Danny to me, "both of you pack up your books and get straight to the principal's office! And consider yourselves banned from the library for the rest of the year."

Great Cat Ambushes.

Both of us? The rest of the year? Great. There goes my history assignment. And my English reading. And my social studies research. How could Danny be so dumb?

I gather up my books. There's no use arguing.

Mrs. Wharton escorts us to the door and slams it behind us.

cat's food

"Danny," I say, turning to face him, "you are a prize bozo. Did you really think . . ."

But I don't finish my question. Danny's not there.

"Dan? Where are you?"

I hear a giggle and then a tremendous belch in my right ear. It's so loud it almost ruptures my eardrum.

He He
Great HUMAN Ambushes.

I spin around.

"Danny?"

I'll call the author...

121

But there's no sign of him — no visible sign anyway — just the sound of his crazy laughter echoing down the empty corridor.

The principal can wait. I'm going straight to the nurse's office.

I'm feeling a little faint myself.

A TerrIBLE christmas and a CRappy new year

Sunday afternoon.

Jen's Christmas cards are sitting on the table. All fifty thousand of them in three big stacks. The envelopes aren't sealed, so I figure that means she wants me to open them and have a look.

I open the top envelope. The card has a picture of a big jolly Santa's face on it.

The message on the inside reads: *Dear Kerrie, Wishing you a Merry Christmas and a Happy New Year. Love, Jen.*

Very original . . . not!

The second card has exactly the same picture on it.

And inside, Jen has written exactly the same greeting: *Dear Sandra, wishing you a Merry Christmas and a Happy New Year. Love Jen.*

She has written the same thing on every card. The only thing that changes is the name of the person she's sending it to.

SANTA
BOARS!

There's only one thing to do.

I grab some Wite-out, a black marker, and get to work.

I don't have much time. Jen will be wanting to catch the six o'clock mailing.

On the first card, I draw heavy dark eyebrows over Santa's twinkling eyes. He's not looking quite so jolly now.

But still, it's not enough. I draw a scar running from the corner of his right eye to the corner of his mouth. I black out one of his front teeth and give him a black eye. And just for fun, I add a couple of Frankenstein bolts to each side of his neck. That's better. Completely psycho.

Now for the greeting on the inside. Merry Christmas? I don't think so. I change the M on *Merry* to a T, cross out the Y and add IBLE to the end. And a happy new year? Not if I replace the H on *Happy* with CR. Much nicer ... A TerrIBLE Christmas and a CRappy New Year.

I go through the rest of the cards, changing the greetings and adding eyebrows, scars, mustaches, nose rings, eyebrow rings, tattoos, antennae, and Martian ears to the Santas. By the time I'm finished, no two Santas are alike. The only thing they have in common is that if you saw any of them coming toward you on the street, you'd turn and run the other way.

I put each card carefully back into its envelope so it doesn't look like they've been messed with.

And, as if brightening up her Christmas cards isn't enough, I even take the trouble to find Jen and ask her if she'd like me to run them down to the mailbox for her.

She asks me if I'm feeling all right.

I tell her that Christmas is a time for giving and that doing things for her makes me happy.

She accuses me of sucking up because it's Christmas.

If she only knew . . .

for me!
How cute.

The mailbox is on the other side of the hill.

There are so many cards I almost get repetitive stress injury putting them in the box. But at last they're all sent.

I'm feeling pretty happy with myself.

Jen's friends all think they're so sophisticated. I can just imagine the looks on their faces when they see their mutant Santas. They'll think Jen has lost her mind. Maybe they'll kick her out of the gang for being so childish. That would be excellent. Then maybe she could get some new friends. Some nice ones.

SNACK
FOR
SANTA

rip
ire chimney

SANTA
TRAP.

And then an awful thought occurs to me.

What if Jen's friends retaliate? What if they start sending cards back to her wishing *her* a terrible Christmas — or worse? I wouldn't put it past them.

It's not going to take Jen long to figure out

that I had something to do with it.

And then she'll punish me by giving me a horrible present or, even worse, no present at all.

Maybe this joke wasn't such a great idea. . . .

I have to get those cards back out of the mailbox!

Luckily, the mailbox has a handle. Since it's Christmastime, the box is probably so full that Jen's cards will be right on top. Getting them back is going to be easy.

I pull the handle toward me and slide my arm into the mail slot. Standing on the tips of my toes, I ease the handle away from me and try to curl my arm down into the box. But it doesn't work. My arm is jammed against the back of the mail chute. My fingers are no-where near the letters. There must be a better way.

I could get a fishing line with a hook on the end of it and try fishing them out. No, that would take too long.

It's getting late. I'm getting desperate.

Perhaps I could build a fire around the bottom of the box so that it heats up and becomes like a huge oven and incinerates everything inside it.

Or maybe I could grab the hose from the house opposite and fill the mailbox with water. Then the ink on the front of the envelopes would smudge and run and the post office won't know where to send them.

They are both brilliant plans, but neither would be fair to the innocent letters already in the box. I don't want to stop them getting through — I just want Jen's letters back.

I hear a squeal of brakes behind me.

I turn around. It's the mailman!

"Am I glad to see you," I say. "I just mailed some letters, but I think I forgot to put stamps on, and I was wondering if you could get them back for me."

"Sorry," says the mailman, "I can't help ya. I'm not allowed to do that."

He puts a sack underneath the door and turns the key.

Hundreds of letters flow into the sack.

"Besides, it'd take ages to find your letters," he says. "Go down to the post office. They might be able to help."

"But I can't get there now," I say. "It's too late."

He shrugs. "Too bad."

"Please?" I say. "It's a matter of life and death."

"So's my job," says the mailman. He gets into his van and zooms off.

So much for Christmas spirit.

AMAZING
EYE
TRICKS#5 *
ANSWER.
At first
sight it
seems that
circle 'b'
is the
bigger.
But
actually
'a' is
bigger.
It looks
smaller
because
it's
further
away.

* See pg 137.

I don't see much of Jen for the rest of the week, until Friday afternoon. The mail arrives late. There's the usual boring letters for Mom and Dad, a couple of cards for Jen and, as usual, nothing for me.

I go to Jen's room and knock on her door.

"Yes?" she says.

"Some letters for you," I say.

She opens the door. Her eyes are puffy, as if she's been crying. I hand her the envelopes. She takes them without a word and closes the door.

A few minutes later, I hear loud sobs

What to
wear
for work
experience!

The
Accountants.

oh... oh !!

coming from her room.

I can guess why. It's just as I feared. Her friends are sending her horrible cards. I should confess, but how can I?

And what if Santa finds out? He only comes to *good* boys and girls. What a dumb prank to play right before Christmas.

Due to lack of space, the best practical joke ever has been moved to Pg 24.

It's the night before Christmas. I'm in the living room. It's dark, except for the blinking of the Christmas tree lights.

I've just put out a glass of milk and some chocolate-chip cookies for Santa, like I do every year. I've laid a pillowcase on a chair and written my name on it in black marker so he'll know it's mine. I'm just adding a few last-minute items to my letter to Santa when I hear the unmistakable sounds of jingling and reindeer hooves on the roof.

He's early!

I quickly fold the letter and stuff it into the envelope.

But before I can get out of the room, there is a huge crash. And then a stream of angry cursing. Well, I think it's cursing. Some of the words are new to me, but they sound like the sort of thing I'd get into trouble for repeating.

What to wear for work experience: At the Dentists

A cloud of black soot explodes from the fireplace, followed by Santa.

At least, I *think* it's Santa. . . .

There's no big white beard or red suit, and he's as skinny as a rake. He is clad in black leather with chains and silver studs. His face is covered in a dark three-day-old beard and one of his front teeth is missing. He has a black eye and a scar running from the corner of his mouth to his ear. And worst of all, little Frankenstein bolts are coming out of his neck.

HOURS OF FUN:

He seems strangely familiar. Where have I seen this man before?

Saw all your family's Xmas presents in half.

And then I remember.

I created him. He's one of the mutant Santas from Jen's Christmas cards.

"Stop right there, you little weasel!" he booms. "It's time all *good* children were in

131

bed! What are you doing still up?"

"I-I-I was in bed," I say, "but then I remembered I'd forgotten to put out some cookies and a glass of milk for you."

"Milk?" he snarls, and then spits into the fireplace. He picks up the glass and throws the milk in my face. "Milk? What sort of a wuss do you think I am! Got anything stronger?"

"There's maybe a Coke in the fridge," I say, wiping the milk from my eyes.

"I mean even stronger! It's cold out there! And as for these . . ."

Santa picks up the chocolate-chip cookies in his bony hands and crumbles them into dust.

"These are for kids! I travel all the way from the North Pole, and you think a few cookies will satisfy my hunger. I want a steak! Medium rare! Now!"

"I'll see what I can do," I say. I run to the kitchen and open the freezer. There are no steaks. All we've got is veggie-burgers. Completely frozen. I guess they'll have to do. I grab the box and go back to the living room.

Santa is scratching his butt.

"Well?" he says.

"How about a veggie-burger?" I say, offering the box.

He shakes his head.

"You're an idiot!" he says. "I don't know why I waste my time. What's that in your other hand?"

I'm still holding my letter to Santa.

"It's a letter for you. . . ." I say. "With a few of the things I was hoping for. . . ."

"Give it here!" he says, striding over and snatching it out of my hand.

But he doesn't read it. He wipes his nose with it, crumples it into a ball, and throws it into the fireplace.

He sniffs loudly and reaches into a black duffle bag that's slung over his shoulder.

"Okay, Mr. Vege-bloody-tarian! Since you like vegetables so much, this is for you. Catch!"

He throws me a small silver ball.

It stinks.

"Open it," he says.

I peel off a bit of the foil. The smell gets worse.

"Keep going!"

I keep peeling the foil. It's a potato. Dark-gray. Moldy. Stinking.

"Now," says Santa, "eat it!"

And he laughs and he laughs, and that's when I wake up — with a horrible taste in my mouth — wishing I'd never played that stupid childish practical joke on Jen.

Christmas is now only five days away. I've had the rotten-potato dream the last three nights in a row. I'm too scared to sleep. I've got to tell Jen what I've done.

I can hear her talking in the kitchen. I get out of bed. I've got to confess.

I open the kitchen door. Jen is yelling. She sees me and slams the telephone down.

"What do you want, you little snoop!" she snaps. She's holding a card. There's a ripped envelope on the floor.

"Nothing," I say and go straight out. She's had another fight with another one of her

134

friends. She'll probably be friendless for the rest of her life.

And it's all my fault.

It's the night before Christmas. There's a large box wrapped in gold paper underneath the Christmas tree. I hadn't noticed it until now. My name's on the card. And it's from Jen! I hold it up to my ear and shake it. No clues. I peel a bit of the tape away from one end of the paper to try to get a glimpse of what it is.

"Oh, hi," says Jen. "I see you've found your present."

Caught red-handed. I drop the present and turn around.

"Yes, I mean, no, I wasn't doing anything," I stutter.

"It's okay," she says. "It's your present. Merry Christmas."

"Thanks, Jen."

But instead of making me happy it makes me feel even more guilty.

I betrayed her trust.

I defaced her cards.

All her friends hate her, and it's all my fault.

It's now or never.

"Um, Jen, this is probably a really cool present and all, but I really don't deserve it. You see, I changed your cards . . . and I've been feeling really bad about it. . . ."

"So it *was* you!" she says. "I thought so!"

"I know it was dumb," I say. "But . . ."

"Dumb? No way! It was brilliant!"

CORPORATE
SANTA

"Huh?" I say, so surprised I almost fall over. "But over the last couple of weeks you've seemed really upset. I thought it was my fault."

"Oh that," she laughs. "I broke up with Rob, but it's no big deal. We made up last night."

"So, you actually liked the cards?"

"My friends loved them!" she says. "You've started a real craze. Come and see!"

She takes me to her bedroom.

This is a very special privilege. She once told me that if I ever came in here she would personally pull out each and every one of my teeth with a rusty pair of pliers — without anesthetic.

She points to an enormous bunch of cards on her windowsill.

I can't believe my eyes.

On each of the cards there is a different sort of Santa. A sneering punk Santa with a safety pin through his nose. A long-haired heavy metal Santa playing a guitar solo on his reindeer's antlers. There're grunge Santas, hip-hop Santas, hippie Santas, Frankenstein Santas — even a dreadlocked reggae Santa. Wow! Who would've ever thought Jen's friends had a sense of humor?

If you would like more AMAZING EYE TRICKS write to "AMAZING EYE TRICKS" P.O. BOX EMƎШ ●L B■ DUBBO NSW 2830

"Just promise me one thing," says Jen. "Don't tell anybody *you* changed the cards. See, they all think it was my idea and I'd kind of like to keep it that way."

"Okay," I say, "as long as you promise me something."

"What's that?"

"Don't breathe a word about this to Santa."

Jen puts a finger up to her mouth. "My lips are sealed," she says.

HO HO

TOYS

SANTASTEIN'S MONSTER.

I was a Xmas Bon-Bon and I didn't even get a PARTY HAT... or a whistle !! That's it !! I've had enough !!! THIS IS THE END !!!

END

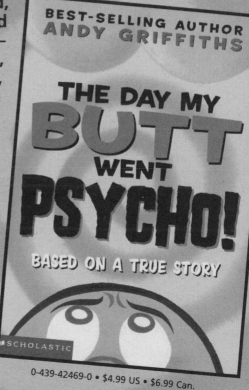